THE HERO I CAN'T RESIST

HOPE FORD

The Hero I Can't Resist © 2025 by Hope Ford

Editor: Kasi Alexander

Proofreader: Nicole Graf

Cover Design: Cormar Covers

Cover Model: Beau Finney

Cover Photographer: Michelle Lancaster, @lanefotograf

CHAPTER 1
ZACH

The last time I saw her, she was a kid. She was a tomboy who trailed after her five older brothers and swore to anyone that would listen that she was going to marry me someday.

I was a twenty-something-year-old and was too busy and too dumb to pay her any real attention.

Now her older brother, my best friend and business partner, wants me to protect her.

"Check your phone," Logan orders me.

I hesitate. My gut has never steered me wrong, and right now it's screaming that this is something big and not to be taken lightly. I should hand this job off to Alex. He's solid. He's a good bodyguard and has plenty of military experience.

Even though I know I shouldn't, I open the video Logan just sent me, and immediately I forget how to breathe.

The woman staring back at me is not a kid. She's a grown, curvy woman. She has her hair twisted up in a messy knot, flour on her cheek, and she's giggling at something off camera. For the first time in my life, I can't look away from a woman.

A thousand questions go through my head, but I know I can't ask Logan any of them. He's overprotective of his sister.

I can just imagine how it would go if I asked him if she was single.

"Zach," Logan says.

I force my eyes off my phone and look at my friend. "What does she need protection for?"

Logan growls. "She's been doing these silly videos, and now she has a stalker."

My heart starts to race, my blood starts to boil, and I'm fighting to remain calm. I start to ask and then stop and clear my throat before trying again. "What do you mean a stalker? And what is this?" I ask, holding up my phone.

Logan shakes his head and waves his hand around. "It's ClipClap."

I am trying to keep the frustration out of my voice, but it's getting hard. "Logan, I know it's ClipClap. I know what ClipClap is. I mean, what is it? Does she do videos like this all the time?"

He rolls his eyes. "It's her job… I mean, that's how she makes her money, and no matter what my brothers or I say, she won't quit."

I cross my arms over my chest. "What do you want me to do? Find the stalker and neutralize him?"

He blows out a breath. "If only it was that easy. I've had the team working on it, and they said that whoever it is has a VPN set up, and we can't trace the IP address."

I turn away from Logan and walk over to the big window. Logan knows me, and there's no hiding from him, but the last thing I need is for him to know I am attracted to his sister. "So what's the plan?"

I can hear the frustration in Logan's voice. "I have to finish this last mission for Walker. I don't have a choice, but I can't just leave my baby sister unprotected."

I'm taking the job. I took one look at her and decided that, but I don't want to seem too interested. "Logan, we're just getting Stronghold started. We have so much to do and—"

"Miller is paying the bill. He put up two hundred and fifty thousand dollars to keep our sister safe."

I turn and look at him in shock. I know Miller. He's Logan's older brother, and I knew he had money, but I didn't realize he had that kind of money. "Two hundred and fifty thousand dollars?"

He shrugs. "He's a millionaire. He wanted to invest in Stronghold, and when I told him I wanted to do it on my own, this was his way of keeping our sister safe and helping me out."

I think about my sister Abby. If she was in danger, I would do—or pay—whatever necessary to do to make sure she was safe.

We're a start-up. We really aren't in a position to turn down paying cases, but getting paid for this doesn't sit right with me. "I'm not taking any money. I'll do it for free."

As soon as the words are out of my mouth, I know it was the wrong thing to say. Logan is instantly curious. He tilts his head. "You want to turn down the money?"

I shrug. "It's your sister, man. She's your family."

He nods, crossing his arms over his chest. "That's what I told Miller."

"And? What did he say?"

He chuckles. "He charmed the bank, got the routing number, and deposited the money into Stronghold's account this morning."

Relieved, not because of the money but because we are definitely taking the job, I shrug. "All right. Did you do the intake paperwork, or do I need to do it?"

He shakes his head. "I haven't done it yet."

I walk over to my desk, which is stacked with boxes and paperwork. "Okay, I'll get a packet and head over. Can you send me the address?"

Logan holds his hands up and shakes his head. "I'm going to go over there and talk to her before I go out of town."

I nod, pick up a packet, and walk toward him. "I'll go with you."

He puts his hand up to my chest and stops me. "Not so fast."

I'm tense and on edge because now that I know that Skyler has a stalker, I don't want her to be alone for another second. "What do you mean, not so fast? I can't protect her if I don't go over there."

"I need to talk to her first."

"Logan... What's going on?"

He shrugs. "Look, she's not going to be happy about this. As a matter of fact, it's probably going to turn into a big argument, so I need to break it to her easy."

I'm practically vibrating with a need to get to her. "What's there to talk about? She has a stalker and needs protection. She has to know with five older brothers that you all are going to step in."

Logan starts to laugh. "Zach, I don't think you get it. Sky isn't the same little twelve-year-old you remember. She doesn't just do what we tell her anymore. She's twenty-five and does what she wants."

Twenty-five. She's ten years younger than me. I mean, I knew that, but this is the first time that I've ever done the math. She's too young for me. She's the sister of one of my best friend's. She's off-limits…

"Plus…" Logan starts and then trails off.

I look at him pointedly. "Plus what?"

He clenches his jaw. "Well, so, my brothers and I always gave her shit about the crush she had on you. I'm sure you don't remember that, but anyway, we sort of tormented her about it. Uh, to the point where she flipped out on us, and after that, we promised we'd never bring you up again… So I'm not sure how she's going to take this."

Stunned, I sit down on the edge of my desk. Fuck, she doesn't even want to hear my name. How am I supposed to protect her?

Logan sighs. "Look, it will be fine. Give me an hour. Go home and pack a bag. I'll text you Sky's address, and by the time you get there, it will all be worked out."

"I'll be there in an hour."

Logan takes his keys out of his pocket and strides to the office door. He stops suddenly and turns toward me. He gives me a look. "This is my sister, man."

I swallow. The weight of it all is heavy, but I know the importance of this assignment. Logan knows I do or else he wouldn't ask me. "I know. I'll protect her with my life."

His shoulders sag with relief, but he instantly tenses again. He gestures to me. "Hey, can you do something about that?"

Confused, I ask, "Do something about what?"

He rolls his eyes. "Come on, Fabio. All women turn to goo around you. Turn down the charm."

I choke out a laugh. "Not once in my whole life has anyone thought I was charming."

He waves his hand around. "You know what I mean. Women fall at your feet, pretty boy. I need you to tame it down. Protect my sister."

Normally, I'd tell him to fuck off, but this is his sister we're talking about. "Got it. Like I said, I'll protect her with my life."

Satisfied, Logan nods and holds up a finger. "One hour."

As soon as he walks out of the office, I pull my phone out of my pocket and watch the video in its entirety. Skylar is making s'mores cookies, and when she takes a bite, my dick twitches in my pants as I watch her lick her lips. I'm not sure how I'm going to survive this job, but I knew the second I looked at her that I had to take it. I'm not going to let anyone touch her… no one but me.

CHAPTER 2
SKYLER

"It's not happening," I tell Logan.

He just smiles at me, and that smile grates on every nerve I have. I'm wiping down my kitchen counter, letting my anger fuel me. I'm scrubbing, huffing, and puffing. There's no way I can give Logan what he wants.

He just told me that my other brother, Miller, had hired Logan's company to serve security detail for me. I point a thumb to my chest. "I don't need security. I've called the local police department. They will handle it."

"Sky bug…"

The nickname from my childhood has me drawing up. I raise my hand. "No, you're not going to call me that. I'm a grown-ass woman, Logan, and I can make my own decisions."

He leans a hip against the island counter. "Sis, I don't think you understand. He's making threats on all your profiles. He's hinting that he knows where you live. It's better to just nip this in the bud."

I stare back at him and debate whether I should tell him that flowers were delivered to my house just yesterday. The card wasn't signed, but I have a feeling it's from the man that has been tormenting me online. I don't want to appear weak, but more than that, I don't want my big brother to worry. He's supposed to be going on a mission out of the country today. "Bub, don't worry about me. You need to be focusing on your mission."

He clasps his hands together in front of him and stares at me wide-eyed. "Listen, I will be able to focus on my work if I know you're safe. If you're here alone, I'll worry the whole time."

I lift my hand and shake my finger at him. "Oh no, you can't do that, Lo. You can't guilt me into doing what you want."

"Sky… please. I don't ask much of you, but I'm asking for this. If the asshole isn't caught by the time I get back, I'll take over your protection detail."

I tilt my head and look up at him. I know I'm not going to win this. Logan is just one of five brothers, and if I tell him no, the other four will be here before the afternoon is over. "I'm not saying yes, but what exactly would it entail?"

He heaves himself up onto my kitchen counter, and I lean against the counter across from him. He leans his elbows on his knees. "Well, let's see. We will have someone move in—"

I interrupt him and point at the ground. "Move in here? Into my house?"

He rolls his head and laughs. "Yes, that's how it works, Sky. He would move in here. He would have full access to your phone, emails, social media accounts. Hopefully, this will just last a few days. Or a few weeks max. We find the stalker, neutralize him, and you can go back to your life of, well, doing whatever you do."

And there it is. Logan and the others don't understand my work. They don't realize how much I love baking and that I love sharing it with my audience. They think I'm just playing around. They have no idea how much time goes into it. And they don't have a clue that I make a helluva living doing it.

"Doing whatever I do?" I repeat.

He jumps off the counter. "Don't be like that. Look, I have to leave soon. Can you just do this… for me?"

I cross my arms over my chest. "Who is it? Who drew the short straw and has to come and protect me?"

"We didn't draw names or anything like that. Zach took the—"

"Zach!" I screech. I push off the counter and pace across the kitchen. "Nope. No way. It's not happening. Forget it."

"Sky—"

I hold both hands up, shaking my head, backing away from my brother. He's crazy if he thinks I'm going to let Zach Campbell anywhere near me. The man makes me crazy. I haven't seen him in person in years, but the majority of my childhood I spent crushing on him. When I became a teenager, it was way more than a crush. I was obsessed. I thought about him all the time, searching for things about him on social media or online. It wasn't until I left

Whiskey Run and went to culinary school that I was finally able to let go of it. There's no way he can move in here.

"Forget it, Logan. It's not happening."

I no sooner get the words out and my doorbell rings.

Logan looks at me with guilt on his face. "Sis…"

I feel as if my eyes are about to pop out of my head. "Oh my God, is that him? Is he here? What's he even doing here, Logan? I thought he was working for Walker. I thought he was a silent partner or something."

He stands to his full height and puts his hands in his front pockets. "He completed his last mission for Walker. He's my partner with Stronghold Security, and you're our first case."

"Case? I'm not a case," I tell him.

He comes toward me and puts an arm around my shoulders as the doorbell rings again. "Sis, please. Just do this for me. I can't leave knowing you are in trouble. Zach is my best friend, and he will protect you."

I pause, and Logan walks with me to the front of the house. All I can do is stare at the door and think that Zach Campbell is on the other side. I want to throw up. Heck, I may just pass out. I come to a halt right before we get to the door. "I don't think this is a good idea. Please, Logan, I'm begging you. There has to be another option."

He lifts his chin and lets out a breath. "Sis, I never tell you what my missions are. I don't ever want you to worry, but I'm also not allowed to tell you all the details." He shakes his head. "What I can tell you is this is a big one. It's dangerous, and it's out of the country. I don't know how long I'll be gone, but I do know that it's going to help me if I know Zach is here with you."

And just like that, I know I have to go along with this. I don't want to because it's going to be really embarrassing. It's like I get around the man and make a fool of myself. I want to stomp my feet and refuse to do this, but I know I can't. I clench my eyes shut, and when I open them, there's no hiding the worry from my voice. "I love you, Logan Brody. I'll go along with this even though I don't think it's necessary, but I need you to promise me that you'll come home."

He hugs me tightly. "I promise, sis."

As soon as he pulls away, he opens the door. I can't stand here. I'm not ready to face Zach Campbell. As my brother greets Zach, I'm gone, almost sprinting through my house back to the kitchen. I need to bake. That always makes me feel better.

CHAPTER 3
ZACH

The door opens, and I'm holding my breath, excited to see Skylar. It took me no time to pack, and the rest of the time I spent watching more of her videos.

Fuck, she's amazing.

I hurried over here, wanting to see her, to hear her giggle and watch her bite her lip when she concentrates. But instead of seeing Skylar, I'm looking at Logan.

He looks worried, and my stomach drops. "What is it? What's wrong?"

He ushers me inside. "Nothing. She took it as well as I expected."

"But she agreed," I insist. There's no other option. I'm not leaving here.

He nods. "Yeah, she agreed."

I drop my bag by the door and look around. When I pulled up to the small house with the white picket fence, my heart started to race. In the past, I would have been freaked out by the cozy feeling this place invokes in me, but not today. No; right now, I feel at peace.

I look around her home, and it's a perfect reflection of her. The lighting is soft, throws tossed over the back of the couch, stacks of books, warm wood, and it smells of vanilla and cinnamon. Every bit of it wraps around me and fills me with a warmth I haven't felt in a long time.

"Where is she?" I ask.

Logan looks around the empty living room. "Uh, probably in the kitchen. That's where she spends most of her time."

I look at him expectantly, and he turns. "Come on."

I follow him through the house feeling incredibly tense. I want to shake my hands to try and calm myself. As soon as we walk into the kitchen, I see Skyler, and I can't look away. She's even more beautiful in person. Her brown hair is in a knot on the top of her head, just like it is in most of her videos. Seeing her here in person, I want to reach out, undo the knot, and let her hair fall down around her shoulders.

She's staring at me with wide blue eyes, and I take a few steps closer. "Hey, Skyler."

She lowers her eyes to the dough in front of her. "Hello, Zach."

Logan looks between me and his sister. "Uh, I'm sorry to run, but I have a plane I need to catch."

Skyler pulls her fingers out of the dough and walks over to the sink. She has her back to us as she washes her hands, and I let my eyes travel down her body. Her curves draw me in, and I put my hands together in front of me to hide my growing arousal.

Drying her hands, she walks into her brother's waiting arms. As they hug, Logan kisses the top her head and whispers, "It's okay, sis. I'll be home before you know it."

She sniffs and pulls away, nodding her head. "You better."

He grips her shoulders. "I will." He gestures to me.

"Please do what Zach asks you to. Let him do his job."

She nods but never vocally agrees.

I come to stand next to Skyler and pat him on the shoulder. "We'll be fine here. Take care of yourself, Logan."

He nods, looks between me and his sister, gives me a warning glare, and then hugs his sister again. "Okay. Love you, sis. Tell our brothers I love them too."

Skyler sniffs, and I walk with Logan through the house. After more goodbyes and instructions, I shut the door behind him. I lock it and then go through the house, testing all the locks on the windows, saving the kitchen for last.

I needed the time to get myself together. When I finally walk back into the kitchen, Skyler is back working on the dough, and she doesn't even look at me when I come in.

I stand across the counter and watch her. She's completely in her element, and it's mesmerizing watching her work. Does she know how beautiful she is? She has to.

"Skyler."

"Yep," she answers quickly, kneading the dough with more intensity.

"We should talk, don't you think?"

She shrugs. "What do you want to talk about?"

When I don't answer, she glances up at me, blushes, and looks at her hands again.

I pull up a stool and sit down so we're almost eye to eye. "What are you making?"

"Sugar cookies."

I nod and quietly watch her. She shapes the cookies, puts them on a pan, and then slides them into the oven. She sets the timer and then crosses her arms over her chest. "Okay. What do you want to know?"

Everything, I almost mutter, but I know that would come off creepy, so I stick to why I'm here. "Everything about your stalker."

She frowns. "Okay. Well, let's see. His handle on social media is 'bakersking.' He pops into most of my live feeds. He leaves messages on all my videos. And…"

When she stops, I tense up. "And what?"

She lets her shoulders droop and walks over to the trash can. She opens the lid and points down inside it. "I got these yesterday."

I walk over next to her and see the bouquet of daisies. "Did he deliver those to you… here?"

She blinks up at me, and for the first time, I sense that she is fearful even though she's trying to act like she's not.

She shakes her head. "No. He didn't. Someone else delivered them. The card is right there. I figure I'd give it to the policeman that is supposed to be handling this. But he says there's nothing he can do unless the guy actually does something."

I grab the card off the counter and read it. "Blue is my favorite color. Like your eyes."

The writing gets blurry as rage travels through my body. This motherfucker watches her, lusts after her, makes her feel unsafe. I will fuckin' end him.

I turn to Skyler. "We need to talk."

She shrugs and looks at the timer before gesturing to the table in the corner of the room. "Have a seat. The cookies will be out in a minute."

I stomp over to the table, pull out the chair, and sit down. I'm trying to calm myself, but inside, I'm fuming.

I turn the card over in my hand. Petal + Leaf.

I pull out my phone, take pictures of the front and the back of card, and send them to Alex Colby. He's coming to work with us at Stronghold Security, and if anyone can get the details on who purchased the flowers, he can. He has almost as much military experience as Logan and I do.

She works around her kitchen, and I just sit here and blatantly watch her. Neither one of us talks, but it's a comfortable silence.

Eventually the timer dings, and I watch Skyler take the pan out and set it on the stove. She pours milk into two glasses and carries them over to the table. Then she plates some cookies and brings those over too.

After sitting down across from me, she crosses her hands on the table. "I don't need you to protect me."

I sit up a little taller. "I'm not leaving."

She sighs and shakes her head. "Zach, listen. I agreed because I don't want Logan to worry about me while he's gone, but I really don't need a bodyguard. I can take care of myself."

I bite back the urge to give in. I'm not giving in.

She tilts her head to the side. "Look, I don't want you to waste your time or your resources taking care of me."

"Miller already paid."

Her eyes widen, and she throws a hand up. "I'm sure I'll be getting visits from all my brothers over the next few days."

I just sit here, watching her. If she thinks I'm leaving, she's mistaken. There's nothing that will force me out of here. Whether she wants to believe it or not, she's in real danger, and over my dead body will I let someone hurt her.

My silence doesn't sit well with her. She bangs her hand softly on the table. "Zach, will you please listen to reason? This is a bad idea. You can't stay here."

CHAPTER 4
SKYLER

As soon as I say the words, I know exactly how it sounds. My mind travels back to the days when I was crazy in love with this man. My cheeks turn red just thinking about the twelve-year-old girl that told everyone Zach Campbell was going to marry me someday. I cringe just thinking of all the times I wrote out *Skyler Campbell* in my notebooks.

I lower my eyes to the table. "I want you to go."

He acts as if I didn't say a thing. He picks up a cookie and takes a bite. He moans and then shoves the rest of it into his mouth. "Damn, that's good."

"Zach, did you hear me? You can't stay here."

He shrugs and picks up another cookie. "I'm staying."

"There has to be someone else."

He sits back in his chair and crosses his arms over his barrel of a chest. He tilts his head to the side and looks at me. "What's wrong with me?"

I clench my eyes shut. Can this get any more embarrassing? "There's nothing wrong with you, but you have to see why this is a bad idea."

He leans toward me. He's across the table, but he's a big man, and I feel his closeness like he's touching me. "Why is this a bad idea?"

I hold my hands up. "You know what? Forget it. You want to stay here, you're welcome to, but I figure you're going to be bored out of your mind by tonight and then you'll be going home."

He just smirks at me, and that look makes me crazy.

I stand up. "Okay, well, I need to get ready. I have a taping in thirty minutes."

He stands up too. "Where is the taping?"

I walk toward the kitchen. "Right here."

He follows right behind me. "All right, what can I do?"

I go to the sink to wash the few dishes there. "Nothing."

I'm drying my hands when I turn around, and if I didn't know better, I would think I just caught Zach Campbell looking at my ass.

He slowly raises his eyes up my body, and that same smirk is still on his face. "Uh," I stutter, "are you planning to sleep here?"

His eyes darken, and he licks his lips, and that's when I realize how that sounded. "I mean, are you staying here in the guest room? Don't feel like you have to. As a matter of fact, maybe this can be a nine-to-five protection or something."

He walks over to me and puts his hands on the counter, one on each side of me, caging me in. "Okay, let's get a few things straight."

I suck in a breath, my head tilted backwards so I can look up at him. He's so close I can smell his woodsy cologne. God, is it cologne, or does he just smell like that?

He leans down, and his nose is just a few inches from mine. "Until we find the creep, you and I are going to be joined at the hip. I'm staying here in your house. I'm going to monitor your emails, messages, and visitors. Until I know you're safe, I'm not going to let you out of my sight."

Speechless, I just stare up at him.

He looks almost pained as stands up to his full height. He's still close but no longer leaning into me. His hands are fisted at his side. "Sky."

I croak. "Yeah?"

"Do you have a boyfriend?"

My throat feels as if it's closed up. "What?"

His jaw tightens. "It's best if you tell me now instead of me finding out later." He backs up, leaning on the counter behind him. "You know what? Let's just make this easy. Break up with him."

My mouth drops open. "Wait. You want me to break up with my boyfriend?"

He growls. "Yes. Now. Today."

I blink in surprise and then shake my head. "Uh, if I do have a boyfriend, you can't just tell me to break up with him."

He gives me one terse nod. "Yes, I can."

Confused, I shake my head. "What is happening right now? Look, I agreed to protection, but I'm not going to just let you boss me around."

"Do. You. Have. A. Boyfriend?" he asks, enunciating each word.

I shake my head. "No, but that's not the point."

He points toward the front of the house. "I'm going to finish checking windows. I'll let you get set up."

I stare at him open-mouthed as he walks out of the kitchen. What just happened? I swear for one second there, it was like Zach was jealous. But just as quickly as the thought comes, I shake my head. Nope, there's no way. I'm sure it's wishful thinking on my part.

My phone dings, letting me know I have fifteen minutes until my live starts.

I finish cleaning up, wiping down the counters, and then I get all the ingredients out for the cupcakes I had planned to make tonight.

I've done this so many times, I don't even have to think about it. I grab all the ingredients, thinking about Zach.

Salt, baking powder, egg, brown sugar, oil, vanilla, baking soda, butter, sour cream, powdered sugar, peanut butter, flour, heavy cream, milk, and a bag of peanut butter cups. I measure everything out and put them in aesthetically pretty bowls so I can just dump it all in on the live.

My five minute till live time dings.

I set up my camera, make sure the lighting is up and ready, and then turn on my microphone. I spend the rest of my time pacing back and forth until it's time to go on.

I'm wondering where Zach is, but I'm thankful that he hasn't made his way back to the kitchen. I'm not sure if I can do my show with him watching.

Right on time, I turn the camera on and push the Go Live button.

"Hey, Cookie Crew, I'm back, and do I have something sinfully sweet for you tonight. I looked at all your votes, and I'm excited to say that peanut butter cupcakes had the most."

I pump my hands in the air as if I'm cheering.

Right at that moment, Zach walks into the kitchen.

I try not to stumble, but there's no way I can't look at him. It should be a sin to be as handsome as he is.

I force my eyes to the camera. "So let's get started. As you know, we're going to get everything stirred up and in the oven, and then we're going to chat."

I go through measurements of each of the items, dumping the ingredients into the bowl.

Zach is staring at me, but I don't dare look at him.

I smile into the camera, walk them through all the steps, and once I'm opening the oven and putting the cupcakes in, I finally take a breath.

I lean down to read the comments. I read one, answer the question, and then move on to the next. This part used to scare me, but now it's almost as much fun as the baking.

"Hey, Leena, thanks for joining in." I hold up the bag of candies. "No, we didn't add these to the mix because we're saving them for after the cupcakes are iced. We're going to put one on each and every cupcake. Yum, amiright?"

Question after question, I go down the line until I see that bakersking has commented. I start to stutter and look over at Zach. It's as if he is completely attuned to me. He knows something is not right because he stands up from the stool he was sitting on.

I skip the bakersking comment and go to the next.

But bakersking keeps commenting.

The more I see his handle, the more I stutter.

Zach comes toward me, and I should stop him, but I don't know how. He comes to stand right behind me, hands on my shoulders, and leans over my phone to read the comments. He tenses, and that's when I realize that I'm live… with Zach Campbell standing protectively over me.

I turn and look him. "Ha, ha, big guy! What's up? I know, I know. You want a cupcake, but you're going to have to wait until they're done."

He realizes his mistake almost instantly. He was concentrating on protecting me and didn't realize what he just did.

He gives me that smile of his, and my knees turn to jello. I smile back at him, but I don't miss a thing. The way his hand squeezes my waist. The reassuring smile that he gives me. Or the way he leans in to whisper, "I'm right here."

He walks away, and I can feel the heat in my cheeks as I look back at my phone. It's blowing up with hearts and comments.

"Ooh, girl, who is THAT?"

"Is that your boyfriend?"

"Is he single?"

"Dang, he's handsome."

"Girl, it's getting hot in here."

I put my hand over my mouth and keep reading. I glance at Zach, but he's staring down at his phone. I look back at my screen. Comment after comment of people thinking that Zach is my boyfriend. Oh my God, this is so embarrassing.

I put my hand on my chest, right over my heart. "Wow, Cookie Crew! That woke you up, didn't it? To answer all your questions, he is my friend. He, uh, was excited about the cupcakes tonight and—"

I stop when another comment from bakersking comes up. *You are mine. No one else can have you.*

I'm just staring at the screen, and for some reason his words fill me with fear. I can feel the blood drain from my face, and I'm frozen.

Zach steps up next to me, rubbing his hand on my back soothingly. I lean into him with a smile frozen on my face. What the hell is happening right now? He looks straight into the camera. "Hey, Cookie Crew, Sky is just being bashful. Or maybe she doesn't want to answer because we haven't talked about it, but I'd be a fool to let this moment pass me by."

He pauses and then puts his hands around my waist. "Sky. I know we haven't been together long."

I gulp. *Oh my God, where is this going?*

He smiles at me and gives me an encouraging nod. "But will you be my girlfriend?"

My whole body jerks. Is this a joke? What is he doing? What's he thinking? Does he not realize how many followers I have? I laugh and try to make a joke out of it. "Zach, do you realize you just asked me to be your girlfriend in front of my two million followers?"

He nods, still smiling. The number of people that could be watching doesn't even faze him. "Yes, what do you say? You wanna be mine?"

I'm saved by the timer going off, letting me know the cupcakes are done. I'm about to get them when

Zach grabs the oven mitt off the counter. "I'll do it."

As he does that, I look at the comments coming in.

"Yes! Say yes!"

"If you don't want him, I'll take him."

"Girl, you're loco if you don't claim that man."

"Wow, he wants you. I can feel the heat through the screen."

I raise up and clear my throat. "All right, Cookie Crew, we're getting off topic."

I show Zach where he can put the pan, and as soon as he takes the mitt off, he faces me and puts a finger on my chin. "Well, what do you say?"

Oh my God, this again? He had the perfect out. I throw my hands up with a shrug of my shoulders. "Sure, I'll be your girlfriend."

I know it's fake. I know it's because he's trying to catch my stalker or scare him off, but the satisfied smile that Zach gives me makes me wish it was more. He leans toward me and kisses my forehead. "Okay, sweetness, I'll let you get back to work."

He looks at the camera. "You heard it here, Cookie Crew. You're my witnesses. She said yes."

I get back to my cupcakes, going through the motions, but the whole time, I'm on edge. Not because of my stalker, who is still watching on the live, but because Zach just claimed me as his girlfriend in front of everyone. There's no doubt about it. I'm not getting out of this without a broken heart.

CHAPTER 5
ZACH

I know I fucked up. I know I shouldn't have gone onscreen, and I sure as hell shouldn't have asked her to be my girlfriend.

I pick up my phone. Logan is on a plane across the country, but I expect a phone call from one or even all four of her other brothers. They're going to be pissed, and I can't say I blame them, but I can't worry about that right now.

I look at the handle for bakersking and screenshot some of his comments. The more I read, the more pissed I get. He's crazy… and he's not going to get anywhere near Skyler.

As I keep reading, I see that he's going off the rails.

He didn't like it when I came onscreen.

"Skyler, who is that man?"

"Tell him no, Skyler."

"You may not know it yet, but you're mine."

"You're mine, and no one else can have you."

The comments get pretty heated, and Skyler's loyal fans start telling him to stop.

Did I do the right thing? I dunno. Is bakersking going to escalate? He might.

I walk into the living room and sit down to finish watching Skyler's show from my phone.

She's recovered from me butting in. I'm transfixed on her icing the cupcakes. Fuck she's beautiful anyway, but doing what she loves, she's practically glowing.

When she signs off, I prepare myself because I know what's coming.

No sooner does she sign off from her show than she's stomping through the house. As soon as she spots me on the couch, she puts her hands on her hips. "What the hell was that?"

I nod. "You have every right to be mad at me right now."

She nods. "Yes, I do. What were you even thinking? This is my job. This is my livelihood."

I stand up. "I know that. I wasn't trying to hurt you, you have to know that. I saw the comments, and I don't know what went through me. I wanted to——"

I stop myself before I say too much.

She starts to laugh. "What? You wanted to do what? Embarrass me? Pay me back for the stupid naïve twelve-year-old I was? Or maybe you just want to see——"

"Stop." I move across the room to her. "Stop it."

She's breathing hard, and I put my hands on her shoulders to try and calm her. "Sky, listen, I wasn't thinking. You want the truth? I saw what he posted, and it went all through me. It wasn't professional what I did, but in that moment, I had to let him know that you weren't here alone, that you had me by your side."

She holds her hand up. "By my side? You didn't just show him you were by my side. You claimed me, you asked me to be your girlfriend!" She blows out a breath, and her voice is strained. "I don't know if you realize it or not, but fans love this kind of stuff. My viewership just exploded."

"That's a good thing, right?" I'm quick to jump in. Dang, something good has to come from my choices.

"Good?" she asks. "Yeah, sure, until you break up with me and people lose their minds, blaming me. There are already people commenting that there's no way I'm pretty enough for you. Some of these people are brutal."

I shrug. "First of all, that's ridiculous. You're beautiful. And second of all, we just won't break up."

She stares wide-eyed at me. She goes to her tiptoes, lifts her hand, and touches my forehead. "I'm sorry, did you hit your head or something? We're not even together."

I'm going crazy. That's all I can think because to me, we're together. Yeah, I haven't seen her since she was a kid. Yeah, I took one look at her in a video on my phone and thought, *mine*. I'm so royally fucked right now.

I release my hold on her and back up. "Look, my job is to protect you, and that's what I'm going to do. And that's in all things. I'll protect you, your reputation, all of it."

Her phone rings, and her eyes widen as she looks at the caller ID. "It's my sister-in-law, Aria."

She answers it, and I wish I could hear the other side of the conversation because it's obvious Skyler is freaked out.

"Shit" is all she says.

I hold out my hand. "Here, let me talk to her."

Skyler must be freaked out because she just hands over her phone without argument. "Hey, Aria. This is Zach. Is everything okay?"

Instantly, she asks, "Yeah, are you packing?"

"Excuse me?" I ask her.

She huffs in frustration. "Do you have a gun?"

"Yes. Do I need it?"

I'm not sure if we're talking in code or what, but I'm on high alert.

"No!" she screeches. "Miller and Penn are on their way over there. They're pissed, and I really don't want you to shoot my husband or my brother-in-law."

I blow out a breath. "They saw the streaming?"

She laughs. "Oh, they saw it, and they're not happy."

"Okay. I'll take care of it."

I'm about to hand the phone back to Sky when Aria demands, "Don't hurt her, Zach. If anyone can, it's you." She blows out a breath. "And if you do, you won't have to worry about the Brody brothers because I'll get to you first."

I look into Sky's big blue eyes. I'm not sure if she can hear Aria or not, but there's a vulnerability on her face that makes me want to reassure her. "Aria, the last thing I'll do is hurt Sky. I promise you, she's safe with me."

Sky's eyes get even bigger, and she looks at me as if she's trying to figure me out. I hand the phone back to her, and she walks from the room to finish the conversation.

I should probably be nervous. Miller and Penn are two guys I don't want to mess with. Heck, you don't want to get on the bad side of any of the Brody brothers. But I'm not bothered by this. I'm looking at it as two of the many obstacles I'm going to have to overcome to earn Sky's trust.

I keep waiting for Sky to come back to the living room, but I don't see her until there's a heavy knock at the door. She meets me there, and I stand in front of her. "I'll get it."

She points at the door behind me. "We know it's my brothers. Maybe you should go do something while I talk to them."

I shake my head. What kind of men has she been with that would just walk away and let her deal with a problem? Just the thought has me scowling. "Let me take care of this, Sky."

She seems shocked. "You want to deal with my brothers?"

I nod. "I think it's best."

She laughs. "Okay, have at it, but don't say I didn't warn you."

She steps to the side, and after looking out the peephole to make sure it's her brothers on the other side, I undo the lock and open the door.

Miller doesn't hesitate when he sees me. He pushes me backwards into the house, up against the wall of the entryway. I don't react. I don't blame him, really. Her brothers have always been protective of Sky, so I expect nothing less.

I let Miller get a punch into my stomach. I'm not going to lie; the hit hurts.

I normally would react, but I know I can't. Not if I ever want Sky to be mine.

She yells at Miller and comes to grab her brother, trying to pull him off me, but Penn jumps in, wrapping his arms around her middle.

Rage goes through me. I know it's her brother, but I can't contain it. My voice is laced with a threat. "Let her go, Penn."

Miller pauses in his attack, and both of the men stare at me. I grit my teeth. If he doesn't let her go, I'm going to fight back. "I'm telling you one last time, let her go."

Penn must see something in my face because he releases his hold on his sister. Even Miller's hands lighten against my chest. Sky is looking up at me in shock, and I have to drag my eyes from hers. "Now, Miller, can we go in the other room and talk for a minute?"

He releases me and without a word walks down the hallway. I stop in front of Penn. "You want to get a hit in?"

He smirks and holds his hands up. "I have surgery in the morning. I can't hit you. I'll leave that for Miller."

I shake my head and look at Sky. She doesn't know what to make of all this. I'm sure she feels like I walked into her world today and turned it upside down. I give her a reassuring look as I walk past her to follow Miller.

He's pacing the kitchen when I walk in. I lean against the counter, feigning a calmness that I don't really feel. I don't know if I'll ever feel calm now, not while there are men like "bakersking" that believe they can terrorize my Sky.

Miller stops, takes a deep breath, and lets it out. He has a dress shirt on, sleeves rolled up, revealing the tattoos on both his arms. He's a millionaire, but right now, he looks like a man about to lose his shit. "I paid two hundred and fifty thousand dollars for my sister to be protected, and you're turning it into a booty call."

I push off the counter and stalk toward him, hands fisted at my sides. "First of all, be very careful how you talk about your sister. Second of all, I told Logan I didn't want to take the money. He said you already paid it, so I told the accountant to pin it for a future case. I'm not taking payment for protecting… Sky." I almost said *my* Sky, and it's good I caught myself because I can't imagine that would have landed well.

Miller is taken aback. "Wait. What?"

I start to repeat myself, and he holds his hands up. "Why would you do that?"

Fuck. How do I even answer that? I decide to just be honest. "Because your sister means something to me. Because I want her safe, and it kills me to think that this guy is terrorizing her."

He walks slowly to me and stops. "What do you mean, she means something to you? Is there something going on here?"

I jut my chin. "Today is the first time I've seen her since she was a kid, if that's what you're asking."

He looks at me with doubt in his eyes. "And what? You decide you need to be the one to save her? This isn't adding up, Zach."

My voice is quiet and tense. "Trust me, I know how the video looked, but I can promise you, none of it was planned. All I can tell you is the truth. I was watching her from the sidelines, and I knew the minute her stalker joined because Sky lost some of her joy. I moved closer to see her phone, not even thinking I could have checked mine. And when I saw his comments, I did what I thought I had to do. I wanted the asshole to know that she had me in her corner. That she was protected. I acted on impulse, but I think it was the right move."

He looks at me through scrutinizing eyes. "You like her?"

My jaw tightens. "I do."

Miller jerks back and throws a hand up. "Fuck, what am I supposed to do with that, Zach? I know you. Hell, I've known you a long time, but this is my sister. This is her safety."

I nod emphatically. "And I will protect her with every breath I have in my body, Miller."

He's glaring at me, looking for the truth. "You hurt her and I'll kill you."

I shake my head. "I won't hurt her."

He tilts his head and looks at me. He wants to say more, but he doesn't. "Even though you didn't take the money, I want you to keep me updated. I want to be sent daily updates."

I pat him on the shoulder. "I got it, Miller. I'll make sure you know what's going on."

He huffs. "Right, I know, this is what you do, but she's—"

I cut him off. "She's your sister. I get it. Nothing is going to happen to her, I promise."

He nods, and without another word, he walks out of the kitchen. I follow him through the house, and he stops by the front door. "Penn, you ready?"

He's sitting on the couch with Skyler, and her eyes are on me as soon as I walk into the room.

Penn stands up. "I'm ready." He's talking to Miller but points at me. "We good here?"

Miller nods. "Yeah, we're good."

Penn smiles, comes over, and shakes my hand. "Take care of her man, or I'll—"

"Kill me? I got it. You're the third Brody to threaten me today. Your wife was the first one."

When I mention his wife, his face tenses, but I'm not sure what to make of it.

Miller and Penn both hug Skyler, and I wait until they're gone before I lock the door.

CHAPTER 6
SKYLER

My brothers leave, and I know Zach and I should talk, but I'm not sure what to say. So much has happened this evening, and I feel like I need to process it. "I'm going to bed."

Zach is watching me closely. "Did you eat dinner?"

I shake my head. "No, but I'm not that hungry."

He scowls. "Sky, you didn't eat any of the cookies or the cupcakes you made either. Eat with me."

I lift my chin in surprise. "You want to eat dinner with me?"

As soon as I say it, I realize how it sounds. I'm acting like it's a date or something. "I mean, do you want me to fix you something?"

He holds his hand out to me. "No, come on. I'll fix us something to eat."

I stare at his hand, and there's a pull in my belly. I'm not sure what's happening, but I know that there's no world where Zach and I make sense. I avoid touching him and walk past him toward the kitchen. "I can heat up lasagna or cook some chicken if you prefer that."

I'm walking past the island to go to the refrigerator when Zach calls my name. "Sky."

I turn, and he's right behind me. Instantly, I put a hand to his chest to steady myself, and his hands go to my waist.

"Hey," he says.

I'm staring at his chest, frozen. Being this close to him, with his scent surrounding me, feeling the warmth and the weight of his hands on me is a little overwhelming. He lifts one of his hands to tilt my chin up so I'm looking at him.

He leans toward me. "Sky, I know you're used to doing this all alone, but you don't have to. Not anymore."

I search his eyes. He's making it sound like he's going to stick around, and the way he's looking at me feels like this is more than just him protecting me.

As soon as the thought forms, I shake my head, pulling from his hold. "What are we doing here, Zach?"

He huffs out a breath and then lifts me by my hips and sets me on the counter. It all happens so fast that I'm shocked speechless.

He cages me in, putting his hands on each side. "So this is what we're going to do. You're going to sit here, and I'm going to fix you something to eat. I want you to relax."

He's waiting for an answer, and only when I nod does he reluctantly back away. He walks over to the refrigerator, and I can't take my eyes off him. His jeans are tight across his butt, and I feel guilty drooling over him, but heck, every part of him is nice to look at. "Do people still call you Fabio?" I blurt out.

He grabs some containers out of the fridge and turns to me holding them. His cheeks are red. "Not much since I cut my hair years ago."

I nod, but I'm sure he's just being humble. I sit on the counter and watch him work. Every now and then, he looks up at me and smiles or asks me where something is. When he has our food heated up, he hands me a bowl of lasagna with a fork.

I'm about to jump down when he puts his hands on my waist and lifts me down, pulling out the stool with his foot and putting me in the seat. He acts as if I weigh nothing when we both know that I eat more of my baking concoctions than I probably should.

"Is this common for you?"

He grabs two waters out of the fridge, sets them down in front of us, and then sits down on the stool next to me. Instantly, he turns to face me. "Is what common for me?"

I smile. "Oh, I don't know. Manhandling women, taking over their kitchens, bossing them around, uh… asking them to be your girlfriend in front of thousands of people?"

He takes a bite of the lasagna, moans, and points at the bowl with his fork. "Did you make this?"

I nod. "Yes, are you avoiding the question?"

He takes another bite and levels me with a look. He's thinking about how he's going to answer. That much is obvious. When he chews and swallows, he shrugs. "I don't think I was manhandling you. I like holding you."

I'm barely able to process that, but he continues. "I just heated up some food. I'll clean up. Does it bother you to have me in your space?"

He doesn't wait for me to answer. "And I'm sorry if I come across as bossy. This is, uh, new to me, and no, I haven't asked anyone to be my girlfriend, let alone in front of thousands of people. You were my first... and I'm glad you said yes."

I put my fork in my bowl and set it down on the counter next to me. "Zach... what is this?"

I watch his massive chest rise and fall. "You mean, this, between us? You feel it too, right?"

My mouth drops open, and I quickly snap it shut. "Feel what?"

He blushes again, and the sight stuns me. Shocked, I ask him, "You're serious, aren't you?"

He takes another bite of food, chews, and swallows. "Yeah, I'm fuckin' serious. I don't know how not to be... not with you."

I can't dwell on this, so instead I answer the question he asked. "No, it doesn't bother me to have you in my space. It's just new… and I don't know what to make of all this."

He nods and eats the last few bites of his lasagna. He grabs my bowl and puts it in my hands. "Finish that, honey. You have to eat."

I take the bowl from his hands, and he gets up, moving to the sink to clean his bowl. I take a few bites, thinking of everything he just said. He doesn't stop at the one dish. He cleans the bowl and pan from the cupcakes I made. I'm enjoying the view, but I know I should go help. I finish my food and am about to get up, but he holds a hand up to stop me. "Here, I got it."

He takes the bowl and makes quick work of cleaning it. When he's done, he turns, leans his back against the counter, and puts his hands on each side of him. "Nothing can come of this. I mean, not right now."

And just like that, the floor shifts beneath me. I was a fool, and I shouldn't have let my guard down. I felt it too. I felt there was something happening between us, but obviously I was just being crazy.

I get off the stool. "Right. Well, I'm going to cover the cupcakes and then go to bed."

I avoid his gaze and put the cupcakes into storage containers. I feel like I've been on a roller coaster. One minute I feel like he's going to kiss me, and the next he's telling me that nothing can come of us.

Still not looking at him, I walk past him, making sure we don't touch. "Well, I'm going to go to bed. The spare bedroom is at the top of the stairs, first door on the right."

He nods. "And yours is right across from it."

When I give him a surprised look, he shrugs. "I went through the house and checked all the windows and locks. You have a good security system."

I blink. "Yeah, my brothers insisted."

His jaw tightens. "Okay." He crosses his arms over his chest. "We going to talk about this?"

I shake my head and fake a yawn. "No. I'm tired, and I think I should go to bed."

He comes to stand next to me. "I have to protect you, Sky. That's what I need to focus on right now."

What else is he going to say? "Right, I get it." I back away from him. "Thanks for doing the dishes. I'll see you in the morning."

"What's your schedule tomorrow?"

I stop at the entrance of the kitchen. "Uh, I have some content to film, and then I need to prepare for this weekend. I have a brand trip."

He tenses. "A brand trip?"

I nod. "Yeah, Whisked Away invited me. It's at a mountain retreat three hours north of here."

He puts his hands on his hips. "Okay, tomorrow, I need access to all your social media, your emails, and Sky… I'm going on the brand trip with you."

I put my hands up and wave my hands. "No, no way. I'll be fine."

He walks toward me. "It's happening, Sky. You wanna go, I'm going with you."

I stomp my foot, and instantly I feel like a child. But I still poke my thumb in my chest. "I'm an adult, Zach. You can't tell me what to do."

He growls. The man literally growls. "When it comes to your safety, yes, I can."

I open my mouth to argue, but being this close to him is too much for me. I slowly back away. "I'm going to bed. We'll talk about this tomorrow."

He leans in the doorway of the kitchen, and I can feel his eyes on me the whole way up the stairs. I'm almost to the top when he calls out, "Sweet dreams, Sky."

I roll my eyes and then walk into my bedroom, slamming the door behind me.

I'm not sure how I'm going to sleep tonight because all I can think about is Zach and how absolutely irritating—and irresistible—he is. This is not going to work. In one night, my life has been turned upside down. And now I'm just supposed to go on with him in my house, sleeping in the room across from me, after he just claimed me in front of my fans, my stalker, and my family. Yeah, there won't be any sleep for me tonight.

CHAPTER 7
ZACH

I'm sitting at the table in the kitchen drinking a cup of coffee when Sky walks in the next morning. She's wrapped in a fluffy robe, her hair is up in a knot on the top of her head, and she's rubbing her eyes. "Coffee. I smell coffee."

I stand up and go over to the coffee pot. "Have a seat. I'll get you a cup."

She's about to argue with me but stops and sits down across from the chair I just vacated.

I take my time pouring the hot liquid. "Cream? Sugar?"

She groans. "Nope. I need it black."

I chuckle and carry it over, setting it down in front of her. "How did you sleep?"

She just grumbles, then blows on her coffee before taking a hesitant sip. I can't seem to take my eyes off her. Even with the creases from her pillow lining her face, she's beautiful. I clear my throat. "Can you give me access to your social and email today?"

She huffs and rolls her eyes. "You're not going to give this up, are you?"

I shake my head. "Nope. Not until you're safe."

I nod and gesture to my laptop on the end of the table. "It's all in there. Everything is in the folder titled Sweet Temptations. You'll have access to my social media and emails through that tab. If you need passwords, it's in the notes folder, titled the same thing."

I grab the laptop, open it, and run a hand across my jaw as it loads. I start with her email first.

The email app opens, and there's a little over three hundred messages that arrived overnight. I glance at her and then start clicking, reading. I'm stunned into silence as I see all the fan mail she receives. So many emails from people thanking her for her videos or the recipes she's shared. Another person thanked her for her support on her live the other night. My heart expands in my chest until it's hard for me to breathe. "Wow."

"What?" she asks.

I gesture to the emails. "This. You really make a difference here, Sky."

She blurts out a laugh. "Thanks, I mean, I know I'm just a baker and—"

I reach over and put my hand on hers. "Don't do that. Don't put yourself down. This is amazing. You've really touched these people."

She blushes and takes another sip of her coffee. Almost like she can't sit still under the scrutiny, she stands up. "I'm going to fix breakfast."

I watch her until she notices me staring, and then I go back to the emails. The next email I open has me sitting a little taller. "Sky."

"Yeah?" she says as she opens the carton of eggs.

"Do you get emails like this one a lot?"

"What's it say?" she asks.

I read, my body coiled with tension. "Hey my sweet princess. You looked good tonight. So good I would like to spread that peanut butter icing all over your—"

"Hey, hey, hey!" she says, face red. "I get the picture. Yes, I get those all the time, but my assistant or I just delete them. It's no big deal."

I pick up the laptop and move closer to her in the kitchen. She's cutting bread and putting it into the toaster, and I set the laptop open on the counter. "Sky, I need to know these things. Every email like this could be a clue into who your stalker is."

She cracks eggs into a pan and avoids looking at me. "I got it, but in my defense, yesterday was the first time I'd seen you in forever, so don't go getting your boxers in a bunch."

I know she's right. I know I'm being ridiculous, but this whole thing is crazy. I've never felt this out of control before.

I carry the laptop back over to the table and keep reading. I take some notes in my phone, sending a text to our IT guy to have him look into a few things.

Sky plates the food and carries it over to the table. She points me toward it. "Dig in."

She brings over two more plates, and I'm about to ask her who the third plate is for when the back door opens.

I stand up, pull my gun from my waistband, and have it pointed at some young guy carrying a stack of pink boxes. I see the Sweet Temptations logo as the boxes fall to the ground.

"Oh my God, Zach, what are you doing? Put the gun down!" Sky screeches at me.

I tuck it back into my waistband. "A strange man just walked in your back door. How did the door get unlocked? Who is this?"

I'm glowering at the man that just walked into Sky's house like he has every right to be here.

Sky starts to walk over to him, and I loop an arm around her waist. "Who is he?" I demand.

I know I'm being an asshole. Sky jerks from my hold. "Zach, you have to chill out." She walks over to him, and my jaw is so tight it feels like it's going to break. "Terry, I'm sorry about this neanderthal. Are you okay?" She looks at me. "You could have killed him."

I glower at her. "If you don't take your hands off him, I still might."

The man is gasping, hand over his chest. "Oh my God..." He points at me and wiggles his eyebrows at Sky. "He spent the night?" He pulls his phone out and starts typing.

"What are you doing? What's he doing?" I ask them both.

Sky puts her hands on my chest to push me back toward the table. I could easily resist her, but I let her lead me away. "He's texting his wife." She looks at the man. "Are you texting Janie?"

He finishes typing. "You know I am. We saw the live last night. She's going to flip."

Sky takes a deep breath, and it's obvious she's completely irritated with me right now. "Zach Campbell, this is Terry Stevens. He's my assistant."

I freeze. "Your assistant? He works for you?"

Sky shakes her head. "We work together. He keeps me organized."

Terry sits down at the table, laying his phone next to his plate. He picks up the fork and starts eating. He moans and then points at the plate with his fork. "You always fix the best eggs. Do you have any more of that apple butter you made?"

Skyler laughs and opens the refrigerator. "Janie still have you eating low carb?"

Terry groans. "Yes, and it's killing me."

She puts down a jar of apple butter in front of Terry and then sits down next to me. They start to talk, ignoring me, and I know she said Terry is married, but I hate the closeness that Terry and Sky obviously have.

I interrupt their conversation and point between the two of them. "How did this happen? How long have you been working for Skyler? How—"

Sky reaches over and puts her hand on mine. Then, as if she just realized what she did, she pulls back quickly. "He's fine, Zach. Logan did a whole background check on him when I hired him." She looks at Terry and points a thumb at me. "This one takes his job a little too seriously."

I open my mouth. I'm about to tell her that this is more than just a job to me but quickly shut my mouth. I need to keep this as professional as I possibly can, and I'm finding it's going to be damn near impossible.

I turn to Sky's assistant. "What's your take on the stalker?"

Sky starts to choke on the eggs she just took a bite

of. I reach over to pat her on the back, and when she's calmed down, I keep my hand on her.

Sky shakes her head. "I don't have a stalker."

I lean toward her. "Honey, he's definitely a stalker. Just in the few emails and messages I've seen, it's obvious he knows your every move." I sit up a little taller. "He had flowers delivered to your house."

Terry, with a mouth full of bread and apple butter, mutters, "He had flowers delivered? Here?"

I nod and pull out my phone. "I need your cell phone number, address, full name, date of birth—"

Sky cuts me off. "How about his blood type and first born?"

She's trying to joke, but I just level her with a look. "That would be great."

She points a finger at Terry. "Look, Terry checks out, and I'm not going to have you—"

Terry interrupts us both. "Hello. I'm sitting right here." He turns to me. "Do whatever you need to do. Just keep her safe."

I nod, giving some respect to Terry. "Thanks."

Terry shrugs and points between Sky and me before asking her, "So, uh, you going to tell me what's going on with you and Zach here? I mean, you know when I go home, Janie's going to ask."

Sky blushes. "Nothing is going on. He works with my brother. He's been assigned to protect me until Logan gets home."

I interrupt her. "Until you're safe, I'm not leaving until you're safe, sweets."

Her face lights up for all of a second, and then she quickly hides it. She clears her throat and points at Terry. "I have the brand trip this weekend. We need to go over details for it."

Terry looks between Sky and me before picking up his phone. "Okay. I'm ready."

They start discussing the weekend, and I take notes. Sky may not be happy about it, but I'm about to be her plus one.

CHAPTER 8
SKYLER

Four days. It's been four days since Zach showed up at my door. Four days of having him by my side, and I'm going crazy.

I wish I could find a huge flaw in him because then maybe, just maybe I could talk myself out of this attraction brewing between us. But the man is making it hard. It's like he anticipates my every need. He's helped me work, cleaned with me, cooked for me, and talked to me, and even though he's asked me a thousand questions, I have secretly loved every minute of it.

But now that we're out in public with people, it's time to rein it in.

"This is not going to work," I tell Zach for the tenth time in the last hour.

His big hand slides across my back, hooks around my waist, and pulls me closer to his side. "It has to."

I open my mouth, but he turns me so we're facing each other, and I lose all train of thought. The man is too good-looking, and he's making me crazy.

I try to look away, but he gently puts his fingers on my chin, holding my face so that I have to look at him. "I'm not leaving your side, sweets."

I grumble, "Quit calling me that."

He tilts his head to the side, looking at me. I hate it because when he does that, I feel so vulnerable that it freaks me out a little bit. His hands move to my shoulders, and he starts to gently massage them. "What's wrong? Talk to me."

I lean in to whisper because for a brand trip, you never know where the cameras are going to be lurking. "Where should I start? We're lying to these people. They all think we're together." I gesture between the two of us. "This is too much."

Zach looks around, and when he spots a door, he grabs my hand and walks us to it. He pulls me outside and leans me against the wall, putting one hand beside my head. "Look, I know this is a lot.

You have all kinds of stress on you, and I don't want to add to it."

I look at him like I don't believe him. Since the second he walked back into my life, it's been one surprise after another. Just like this brand trip. I know he said he was coming with me, but I didn't realize it meant we were staying in the same room and sharing a bed. I've told myself that I need to keep my distance and my heart guarded, but the more time I spend with Zach, the harder that is.

I shake my head. "I just don't understand. We can have separate rooms."

He rubs his hand through his hair. "Look, I know this isn't ideal, but in order to keep you safe, I am not leaving you by yourself."

I look out at the mountains over Zach's shoulder. "And did we really have to tell everyone I was your girlfriend?"

He searches my eyes. "They all knew anyway. All these people watch your channel, and really, is it such a bad thing that they know we're together?"

I avoid his gaze, not trusting myself. He's hinted a few times about this being real, but I just ignore him. I can totally see me throwing myself at him and really embarrassing myself.

Zach shifts so that I have no other option than to look into his eyes. He's trying to figure me out, and his question rattles me. "What's really going on here, Sky?"

I roll my eyes. "You know what, you want to do this, we'll do it, but no one is going to believe it."

He tenses. "Believe what?"

I point a finger between the two of us. "This. Me and you. No one is going to believe we're really together. This is going to create even more drama, and that's the last thing I want. This is my business, Zach. It's my livelihood that we're messing with, and I can't just… muck it all up."

He cups my cheek, and my heart starts to race. His voice dips low. "Do you trust me?"

I nod instantly because regardless of anything else, I do trust him.

For just a second, I think he's going to kiss me. I wait for it. Hell, I lick my lips in anticipation of it. I'm so ready for it that there's a pull in my lower belly from wanting it. And just when I'm about to go to my tiptoes to get closer, I come to my senses. *This is fake, Skyler. This is not real.*

I force a smile to my face and pull away. "Come on. It's show time."

I am about to walk away, but Zach grabs my hand, threading our fingers together. We walk back into the resort and follow the signs for where the dinner is being held.

There's a cooking segment where the chef is showing off all the Whisked Away cooking and baking utensils. We're supposed to be able to watch while enjoying dinner.

I'm sure Zach is going to be bored out of his mind.

We walk in and are welcomed by the staff. I was originally so excited about this, but now there's a dark cloud hanging over it. This strange man, my stalker as Zach calls him, has wreaked havoc on my life for weeks now. But tonight, I'm determined not to think about him.

I'm smiling as we're led to a table with four other people. I give them a wave. "Hey, everyone. I'm Skyler with Sweet Temptations."

Zach puts a hand at my waist. "And I'm Zach, her boyfriend."

I tense but keep smiling as we sit down.

The woman next to me introduces herself and her husband. "Hi y'all! I'm Cindy, and this is my husband, Mark. We own Southern Food."

I nod real big. "Yes, the food blog. I love that. It's so nice to meet you both."

I look to the two women next to Zach, and they're both staring at him. My voice is strained, but I give them a little wave. "Hello."

The one looks at me, but the other keeps staring at Zach. I glance at him, and he's oblivious to it all because his eyes are completely trained on me.

The woman that can't seem to take her eyes off Zach says, "Hello. I'm Patty, and I own Patty's Pudding. This is my best friend, Kathy."

Clueless, I keep a smile on my face. "It's really nice to meet you both."

Finally, the woman looks at me. "You know, Patty's Pudding. It's on TrueFans. I do live recordings of me making pudding nude."

I had mistakenly taken that moment to drink some water, and when she says it, I start to choke.

Zach is on me instantly, patting my back, asking me if I'm okay.

I barely recover before Patty is shoving her business card and her cleavage into Zach's face. "Here you go. There's a QR code if you want to check it out."

He doesn't even reach for the business card. With a smirk on his face, he shakes his head. "No thank you. The only baking I watch is Sky's."

My whole body goes hot. I don't know if it's the fact that he's turning down an obvious flirt or the way he says my name or what it is, but I feel it all over. For the rest of the evening, Zach turns in his seat so his back is to the voluptuous blonde.

The dinner and the show are amazing. I am amazed by all the cookware and utensils and ecstatic when they announce that everyone has a package waiting in our rooms.

We barely get up from dinner and say bye to Cindy and Mark when I'm racing back to the room. I'm bouncing from foot to foot waiting for Zach to open the door, but as soon as we're inside, he halts me. "Wait here. I'm going to check the package."

My eyes almost bug out of my head. "Check the

package? What does that even mean? Check the package?"

He pulls a tool from his bag, and I point at it. "What is that?"

He shrugs. "Bomb detector."

My eyes widen. "Bomb detector? I know this guy is a little crazy, but not like that. He's not going to blow me up."

For just a second, Zach looks regretful. "He's escalating. Since that first night when I was on camera, asking you to be my girlfriend, he's escalated."

I hold a hand up. "Wait. How did I not know that? I haven't seen any messages from him. No emails, nothing."

He juts his chin at me. "I've intercepted them."

I take a step back. "You intercepted them?"

He nods. "Yeah, I don't want you to worry."

I blurt out a laugh. "You don't want me to worry? You're holding a bomb detector in your hand and think that's perfectly reasonable. Yeah, I'm going to worry."

He curses. "Fuck, I'm doing this all wrong. Nothing is going to happen to you, Sky. I promise, I'm going to take care of you."

He turns to walk to the huge box in the middle of the room. I rush to his side. "Wait."

He patiently turns to me.

I put a hand on his shoulder. "I don't want anything to happen to you either." His face softens, and I know I'm giving away too much. "Look, let's just put the box out in the hallway and give it away."

He points at the box. "This box? You want to give it away? The one that we practically raced back to the room to open?"

I shrug. "Well, it's not worth dying over."

He moves the detector to his left hand and then puts his right hand on my shoulder. "I'm sure it's fine. I'm just being cautious."

I nod, and he gestures to the corner of the room. "Go on. Go stand over there."

I firmly shake my head. "Nope. If we're doing this, we're doing it together."

He wants to argue but decides against it. He rubs the detector along the box, and the room is silent as

I wait for something to alert me. This whole situation is a little overwhelming. It doesn't take long before Zach is putting away the machine. "Go ahead. Open it."

I suck in a deep breath and let it out. The joy and excitement from earlier is now gone. I get the first flap open, and Zach apologizes. "I'm sorry. I ruined it for you, and that wasn't my intention."

I shake my head, forcing a smile to my face. "You didn't ruin it. The asshole stalker did."

Zach smirks at me, and I ask him, "What are you smiling about?"

He crosses his arms over his big chest and shakes his head, still smiling. "You must be really mad because you just cursed."

I blush. It's a bad habit of mine, but he's right. I only curse when I'm mad.

I open the box, and Zach helps me take everything out. He's really trying to get my mind off things, and he asks me to tell him about every appliance and utensil and what I'd like to make with them.

I'm trying. I really am. I answer all his questions, and I am excited about the PR package from Whisked Away, but it seems like the week is just taking its toll on me. Emotions are hitting me hard, and I know I'm not going to be able to keep it together much longer.

"I'm going to go shower and get ready for bed."

He tenses but doesn't say anything. I grab my pajamas and toiletry bag and then make my way to the bathroom. I can feel Zach's eyes on me the whole way, and it's only when I get to the bathroom, shut the door, and turn on the water that I finally let the tears start to fall.

I'm a mess. I know I am.

My stalker is going crazy. I'm spending twenty-four hours a day, seven days a week with a man that I've crushed on for what feels like forever. I know I need to stay strong and keep my guard up, but right now, I'm so damn tired, and I just can't.

CHAPTER 9
ZACH

She's crying. I knew it was coming. I could tell in the last hour that she was overwhelmed, and I'm kicking myself for not being more discreet when checking the box. Maybe I'm going too far, but Sky's stalker is unhinged. I found trackers on my truck and her car and removed them both before we left this morning.

There's no doubt that he knows where she is and is probably following her everywhere she goes. I made sure we weren't being followed when we drove here, but because of the nature of her business, the world knows she's here. Every post and image Sky is tagged in from Whisked Away shows the enemy her exact location.

I stand outside the bathroom, listening to her sob softly. There's steam coming from under the door, and I can smell the scent of her lavender soap. My chest feels so tight that all I can do is stand here and try to breathe.

It guts me, and I'm fighting with myself because more than anything, I want to walk in there and hold her.

As soon as the water shuts off, I move away from the door. I check the deadbolt again, making sure it's locked. I pull the edge of the curtains tighter, making sure that no one can see in. It's habit now, double and triple-checking things, but it's a necessary one.

I hear her shuffling around in there, lids snapping open, more water running, and when the door finally opens, I can't stop myself.

I slowly walk toward her. I take the contents of her hands and drop them on the dresser before pulling her into my arms.

She's stiff at first, but I don't let her go. I slide my hand up and down her back, soothing her the only way I know how.

I haven't hugged anyone in a long time, but this feels good. Almost too good. The hitch of her breath hits me hard.

Finally, she melts into me, and before I know it, she's crying again.

I pick her up, and she gasps. "Zach, I'm too big."

I'm holding her bride-style, and I look into her eyes. "Don't say that. You're perfect."

She wants to argue, but she bites her lip and lets her head fall against my shoulder. I move to the chair in the corner. I sit down, holding her tight against me. Her sobs continue, and with each one, my heart hurts a little more. I wish I could save her from this.

I whisper low, "I've got you, sweets. You're safe right here. I'm sorry, baby. I'm sorry you're going through this. I promise I'm going to keep you safe."

She pulls back and looks up at me with wet, glistening eyes. "What about you? Do you promise you're going to be safe too?"

Gutted.

That's the only way I know how to describe it.

My sister and our parents worry about me and

want me to be okay, but this feels different. "Yeah, I'll be safe too."

I've made the promise before to family, but this is the first time that it feels like more than just words. And I know it's impossible to promise someone that you will protect them, but I know more than anything, I will die trying.

As we sit here, looking into each other's eyes, the moment explodes between us. I'm not sure which of us leans in first, but our lips touch, and I feel the kiss go through my entire body. It's like nothing I've ever felt before, and I know I don't ever want this feeling to end.

I tilt her head, deepening the kiss. Her tongue slides against mine, and I tremble. My cock is hard under her hip, and she shifts her weight on me. A groan erupts from within, and I force myself to break off the kiss.

We stare at each other wide-eyed, neither of us saying anything.

I'm the first to speak, and I know it's the wrong thing as soon as it comes out of my mouth. "I'm sorry. I shouldn't have done that."

She tenses in my arms, puts her hands on my chest, and tries to lift herself off me. My arms go around her. "Don't. Don't move."

She shakes her head. "Zach, this is confusing, and to be honest, I'm not equipped to handle it."

I try to understand her. "Handle what?"

She blinks. "You ask me to be your girlfriend but tell me it's for the job. You kiss me and then apologize. I just… I can't do this."

"I want you," I tell her with complete honesty.

She opens her mouth and then closes it.

I know I owe her an explanation. "But no matter how much I want you, now is not the time. I'm here to protect you."

She takes a deep breath and lets it out. "And what? After this… when you catch the guy… what happens then?"

I search her face. "Well, first I'm going to have a talk with Logan and let him know my intentions."

Her voice is a whisper. "Your intentions?"

I nod, cupping her cheek in my hand. "Yeah. I intend to date you and make you mine for real."

If she asks me what that means, I'll tell her. It might scare her off, but she needs to know that this is the real thing. Her hands slide from my chest to my shoulders. "So you're for real about this? You really do like me?"

I hate that she seems like it's so hard to believe. How can she not know how beautiful, smart, and amazing she is? "Yes, I really do like you."

She leans in, and it takes everything in me to stop her. "But we should wait, sweets. We shouldn't do this until you're safe."

She blinks up at me, and I hate seeing the vulnerability on her face. She doesn't have to say anything for me to know that she's wondering if I'm being real. I'll have to prove it to her, and I'll be happy every day to do just that.

This time when she raises up, I release my hold on her.

She walks slowly across the room, and I give myself a few minutes. My body is hard just from having her on my lap, and even though there's no doubt she felt it on her hip, I don't want to draw even more attention to it.

When I've gained a little bit of control, I stand up. "I'm going to shower."

She nods without looking at me.

I grab some things from my suitcase, and before I go into the bathroom, I remind her, "Don't answer the door for anyone, Sky."

She finally looks at me and rolls her eyes. "Yeah, yeah, I got it."

I disappear into the bathroom and stare at myself in the mirror. I look like a man on the edge. Keeping my hands off Sky is going to take every ounce of control I can muster. Her scent is already on me, clinging to my shirt.

I remind myself that she's my best friend and business partner's little sister. I remind myself that I'm supposed to be protecting her, and to do that, I need to keep this professional. I don't like it. I want it all with Sky, and I don't want to wait. But what kind of soldier would I be if I didn't have discipline?

I turn on the shower, spinning the nob to its coldest setting. I quickly get undressed and stand under the spray. On contact, it takes my breath away, but I let it flow over me until I can normalize my breathing.

I make quick work of getting cleaned up, resisting the urge to wrap my hand around my girth and pleasure myself.

I step out of the shower, dry off, and put on underwear and shorts.

I pull my shoulders back, trying to collect myself for what I'm about to walk into. The woman that makes me feel things I've never felt before is on the other side of the door, and somehow, I have to keep her safe… and keep my hands off her.

The toughest mission of my life isn't in some foreign country, in a desert or some jungle. It's in a motel room, trying not to touch the only woman I want.

CHAPTER 10
SKYLER

I stare at the ceiling, unable to go to sleep. The only sound in the room is the hum of the air conditioner, and the sound should be soothing, but it's not.

It's late, and I should be tired, but I'm not. I feel like there's a live wire inside me, and my body is practically vibrating with it. Zach told me he wants me. He told me that he wanted a relationship with me when this is all over.

I told myself not to get my hopes up, but I can't help it. I know it sounds crazy, but it is like all my dreams are coming true. I huff out a breath.

"Go to sleep, Sky," Zach murmurs.

I roll and look over the side of the bed. The room is mostly dark, but I'm able to make out Zach's figure on the floor. "This is ridiculous. You know that, right?"

He raises his arms, putting his hands under his head. There's a sheet on the floor, and I had to insist that he take a pillow. "Sleep. We have another busy day tomorrow."

"Zach. We're both adults here. You can sleep in the bed."

His voice is strained. "I'll sleep on the floor."

I sit up. "Fine. I'll sleep on the floor too. This isn't right. You're here because of me. You shouldn't be sleeping on the hard floor."

He chuckles. "Sweets, this is luxurious compared to some of the places I've slept."

That thought makes me sad. "I'm coming down there, Zach, if you don't come up here."

He sits up, grabbing his pillow. He walks around the bed and gets in on the far side, putting a huge gap between us. I roll to my back and stare up at the ceiling. Even though we're nowhere near touching, I swear I can feel the shift in the air and the current between us.

"I bet this is boring compared to most of your missions."

I think back on everything I know about Zach. He joined the Army when he graduated high school. For the last ten years or so, he worked with my brother for Walker and his Ghost Team. No one ever really talks about what the Ghost Team does, but just the small things I've gotten from Logan, I know they did a lot of dangerous missions and saved a lot of people.

Zach is quiet for so long I wonder if he's going to say anything when he grumbles, "It hasn't been boring at all."

I roll to my side to face him. "Do you miss it? Going on missions?"

He blows out a breath. "Sometimes. I miss the thrill of it, but my therapist helped me see that it was time for me to move on."

I struggle to ask the question. I don't want to ask anything I shouldn't, but I also want to learn everything I can about Zach. "Your therapist?"

He grunts. "Yeah, he helped me see a few things." He pauses, and I see his chest rise and fall with his breath. "I was dealing with survivors guilt. Hell, I still am."

I search my mind, thinking back to what I know about his past. I remember Logan telling me about the bombing a few years ago, but I don't know a lot more than that. All I knew was that Zach was okay. "What happened?" I ask.

I'm holding my breath, waiting for him to answer me. I'm about to tell him to forget it when he starts to talk.

I lie silently, listening to him, trying to hold back the horror as he tells me the story of his past.

"We were on a mission in Afghanistan. It was supposed to be a simple mission. In and out. There was an IED that went off… Fuck, it was horrible. There were seven of us on that mission. Randall died. The other five are permanently injured and scarred. I'm the only one that walked away without a scratch."

I reach across the middle of the bed and put a hand on his shoulder. "Oh, Zach. I'm so sorry."

His muscles flex under my palm, but he doesn't pull away. "I've lived with the guilt for years now and didn't handle it the best way. I took every mission I could. I didn't take any time off—the more dangerous, the better. It's like I wished that something would happen to me… as if that would relieve some of what I was feeling."

When he stops talking, I'm barely holding it together. I lean my head on my hand, hovering over him. "Zach, we may not have seen each other in a very long time, but I know you… I know the man you are. I'm sure you've tortured yourself since the incident, but we don't know why these things happen. There's a reason you were uninjured. We may never know why… but it wasn't for nothing."

He sighs softly, and I continue. "Think about the people you've saved since then. Heck, Zach, there were seven of you, and the men that were injured made it back home. That was you. If you had been hurt too, who's to know if any of you would have made it home."

He rolls toward me. Somehow he finds me in the darkness, landing a kiss on my forehead. "Thank you," he whispers.

"You don't have to thank me. It's the truth." I put a hand to his chest, over his heart. The steady thud under my palm calms me. "I hate you've had to carry this guilt, Zach, and I'm sorry about your friends. I really am. How are they now?"

He puts his hand over mine as if he's holding me to him, wanting my touch. "Well, Davis married my sister. I gave him shit about it for a while, but man, he loves her. He's a good dad to my niece and nephew." He pauses. "Jason is blind, but half the time you wouldn't know it. He gets around and 'sees' more than a seeing person does, if that makes sense. He's married too. As a matter of fact, all of them are. Kanan, Elias, and Colter. They're all happy."

My heart breaks a little because I can hear the wistfulness in his voice. He wants that. It's like I can hear the yearning. "You deserve to be happy, too."

He shudders and answers thickly, "I'm working on it."

I want to slide over and wrap my arms around him. It's like I can feel the sadness coming off of him in waves, and I can't just lie here without doing something.

I scoot toward him and stop.

My breathing picks up, my heart starts to race, but I don't let myself stop.

I scoot closer, and Zach almost sounds panicked. "Skyler… what are you doing?"

I scoot again, and this time, I'm flush against his body. I feel him all around me. I'm trying to control my breathing, but it's hard because every small move, small breath or anything, and I'm even closer. The warmth of his bare chest heats me up. The scent of his soap and all that is him envelops me like a tight hug.

I press my cheek against his chest and wrap an arm around him. He tenses, but I don't stop the hug. I stroke my hand up and down his side. He groans. "Skyler…"

"Zach." I say his name softly.

He doesn't say anything, and I start to feel like this is a bad idea. I'm about to let go of him when all of a sudden his arm goes around me, and he pulls me half on top of him.

"Baby… we shouldn't be doing this. I shouldn't be in this bed with you, and I shouldn't be touching you."

Hope flairs in my chest when he seems to hold me tighter. "Why? Why can't we do this? I mean if we both want it."

He groans again and buries his nose in my hair. He inhales deeply, and I swear he seems like a man on the verge of losing control. "Sky… I'm supposed to be protecting you."

I part my legs, fitting the "v" of my thighs over his. He's hard, and his manhood is pressing against me.

I rock against him. "You will protect me. I know you will."

He pushes me to my back and hovers over me. His hands are locked on mine against the bed, over my head. His eyes are wild as he looks at me. "Who's going to protect you from me?"

I lean my head up. "I don't need protection from you."

He grunts. "If you knew what I wanted to do to you, you'd think otherwise."

My nipples pucker, and I arch my chest, rubbing my hard peaks against his pecs. The sensation travels through my body, and I know I'd give anything, promise anything, to be with him. I pry my hands from his hold and wrap my arms around his torso. With one small tug, I pull him on top of me, and he grunts. "I want you," I tell him. I'm almost pleading with him. "I want this."

He nuzzles my neck, sending chills down my body. "I promised your—"

I turn my head and find his lips. Like a magnet, our lips connect, and the kiss is all-consuming. I lift my legs, wrapping them around his waist, pulling him tighter against me. "Zach, please. I don't want to hear all the reasons why this is a bad idea or why we shouldn't. Just one night, that's all I'm asking of you."

He puts his hand at my waist and then slides it under the band of my shorts. His finger grazes my mound, and I jerk. He slides a digit between my slick, swollen folds, and I let my legs fall to the bed, open wide.

Zach takes full advantage, stroking me. I pump my hips, and he moans. "Fuck, you'd fit so good wrapped around my cock, sweets."

I groan as he strokes my swollen clit. "Zach, please," I beg him.

He sits up on his haunches, jerking my shorts and panties off in a swift motion. He drops my clothes, puts his hands on my thighs, and pushes them open.

He moves suddenly, leaning over the bed, and flips on the light of the lamp. I squeal, throwing my hands over my body, trying to cover myself. He grabs my wrists and holds them between us, eyes locked on mine. "Stop," he demands.

I stop fighting and stare up at him. "Turn the light off, Zach."

He tilts his head to the side and looks at me. He sits down and pulls me to a sitting position. "We need to talk."

I look at him, aghast. "You want to talk? Now?"

He opens his mouth, but I hold a hand up. "If you're going to tell me all the reasons why we shouldn't be doing this, I don't want to hear it."

He grabs my hand and holds it between both of his. "There are a lot of reasons why we shouldn't do this, and I'm sure I'm going to get an ass-kicking for it, but I want you, Sky. So much that I can't fight this."

A lightness falls over me, and I can feel the tightness in my shoulders start to fade. "Okay, then…"

"But we need to talk before this happens."

"I'm on the pill," I breathe out, thinking that we're having the birth control talk. It's not like I'm sure how this happens, but I'm assuming people discuss birth control before having sex. This is my first time, not that I'll be telling him that.

His jaw tightens, and he nods. "That's good because I want to be inside you with nothing between us."

I suck in a hard breath. "Then what are we doing here?"

"This is not a one and done or nobody has to know situation, Sky. This is more than just a fuckin' way to pass time."

I refuse to be taken in with his words. It's lust talking, plain and simple, and he thinks he has to promise me the world or something, but he doesn't. I want this. I wanted this way before I ever should have. But instead of saying any of those things, I gesture to the light. "And do you need to have the light on to do that?"

"Yes."

I scrunch my nose up. "Why?"

He smiles, and the way he's looking at me has my guts twisting in anticipation. "Because I'm going to kiss, lick, and suck every part of your body, and I want to see every nip I make, every flush on your skin, every tremble... fuck, I want to see it all."

I jut my chin at him. "I…"

I can't bring myself to say it. I'm secure in my plump body. I don't have any qualms about what I look like, but I'm not used to showing it off either.

He puts a finger on my chin and lifts so I'm looking at him. "It's your decision. If you want the light off, I'll turn it off. But I want you to know that I love your body. Just looking at you makes me hard, Sky."

He gestures between us, and his shorts are tented from his erection. "Case in point."

I blush and look away after I see the twitching movement. I look into Zach's eyes, and they're darker than usual, filled with desire. In this moment, I make a decision. I want Zach. I've thought about this, and I know if I don't do it, I'll regret it. I grab the hem of my shirt and pull it over my head. Sitting here in only a bra, I know that my curves are on full display. My thighs are thick, my belly softly rounded, but I don't care because he is looking at me like I'm the most beautiful woman he's ever seen.

I suck in a breath, reach behind me, and undo the clasp of my bra. I let the straps slide off my shoulders, and when the lacy cups fall away, I hold my breath.

Zach's eyes lower, and the second he sees my naked breasts, he physically jerks. "Fuck, you're beautiful."

I reach for him then, and it's like an explosion between us. His kiss is ravaging and all-consuming. My breasts are crushed against his chest, and I slide against him, wanting the friction. I dip my hand into his waistband, and he jerks his mouth from mine. "Baby, I won't last with your hands on me."

He pushes me back on the bed and hovers over me, his eyes devouring me. He's not even touching me, but I can feel him everywhere. My body trembles as he cups my breast and then circles my erect nipple with his rough, padded finger. I arch into his touch.

He leans down, and I still myself, ready for it but having no idea how good it's going to feel. His hot mouth suckles me, and my body jerks. I groan as I clench the sheets into my hands.

He's relentless, suckling one breast while kneading the other. And when his hand dips between my legs and he palms my womanhood, I know that in this moment I would do anything this man wants of me. Anything.

CHAPTER 11
ZACH

I need to slow down.

That's what I'm telling myself, but it's impossible. Touching Sky, tasting her, having her naked underneath me is a temptation I can't resist.

A wet pop sounds as I release her nipple. I kiss down her stomach and sit on my haunches between her thighs. I put one hand on each knee and push her legs apart. Her pussy is glistening, and I slide a finger along her slit. Her hips buck, and she lets out a strangled groan.

Her eyes meet mine, and they're wide, curious, and a little alarmed.

I circle her clit with my finger. "I want to kiss you here."

She sucks in a breath and shakes her head. "You don't have to."

My eyes light up. "Have to? Baby, I want to. Fuck, I want to so bad my mouth is watering."

She nods, and I don't hold back. I dive between her legs and slide my tongue through her slit. As soon as her arousal hits my tongue, I'm obsessed. I lap at her before suckling her clit into my mouth. She moans, groans, and writhes under me, but I don't stop. When she pulls at my hair and her legs stiffen, I apply more intensity. It isn't long before she's coming, saying my name.

Her pussy is vibrating with little aftershocks, and I know it wouldn't take much to give her another orgasm.

She's wet, and I don't want to wait another second to bury myself inside her.

As I climb up her body, I pull off my shorts and toss them by the bed. I hover over her, looking into her eyes.

She wipes at my lips. "You have, uh…"

I smile at her. "Kiss me."

She scrunches her nose up but lifts her head to meet my lips. She whimpers as I deepen the kiss, stroking my tongue against hers. My cock is hard, seeping against her belly.

She reaches between us and tentatively wraps her hand around it.

My hips pump into her hold, and I break off the kiss with a grunt.

"Fuck, that feels so good."

Her eyes are wide as she stares up at me. "Are you sure? I mean, uh, is that going to fit?"

I chuckle. "Yeah, baby, I have a feeling that it's going to fit like a glove... like we were made for each other."

Her eyes are glassy, but there's a determined look on her face. "Do you want me to... you know?"

Her innocence is endearing, and I think it's cute how she's struggling to say the words. Any other time, I'd ask her to say it, but I know if she says the words "suck your cock," I'm going to come right here and now.

"I need to be inside you."

She lets her legs fall open, and I position myself at her entrance. She's looking at me wide-eyed as I slowly enter her.

Her hands are against my chest, and she pushes on me, so I stop. "Are you okay?"

She nods. "Yeah, just, uh, go slow."

Already she's gripping me like a vise, and only the tip is in. Slowly, I start to move, and it's not until I'm met with resistance that I stop. I'm watching her closely, and the wince on her face only cements my thoughts.

"You're a virgin," I say, almost accusingly.

She nods, and her body shudders with her breath.

I freeze, the torment of not wanting to move and needing to, battling within me until my arms and legs start trembling. There's sweat on my forehead as I try to pull myself together. I'm about to pull out when Sky locks her legs around my waist, pulling me deeper inside her.

Unable to hold back, my hips surge forward until I'm buried deep inside her. She lets out a small cry, but just as quickly, she adjusts to me, and after taking a deep breath, she lifts her hips, taking me deeper. I groan. "Fuck, I can't stop."

She hooks her arms around my neck. "I don't want you to."

I search her face because the thought of hurting her kills me. "Are you okay? Are you sure?"

She nods. "Yes, please, Zach, don't stop."

I lift my hips and then push back inside her. The friction is intense—fuck, all of it is intense.

Her eyes start to drift closed, but I'm not having it. "Look at me, Sky. I need your eyes on me."

She looks up at me, and I stare into her eyes as I pump in and out of her. She's practically vibrating around me, and I know I'm not going to last much longer. I reach between us and stroke her clit. She's already sensitive, and her pussy heats and floods. The only sound in the room is our heavy breathing, her whimpers, and the sound of our bodies slapping against each other.

"Come with me, sweets."

Her orgasm hits hard and fast, and she clamps down on me like a vise. I can barely pump in and out of her, but my orgasm takes me over the edge, and I pump my seed deep inside her, groaning her name and saying "mine" over and over.

I'm trying to hold my weight off her, but she has her arms and legs wrapped around me, and she pulls me closer. "Don't move. Not yet."

I know she's going to be sore, and the last thing I want to do is cause her any more pain. I pull out and lie next to her, pulling her flush against me. Already I can feel my body reacting to the feel of her, and I have no doubt that I'm addicted.

I wait for the guilt to set in. This is Logan's little sister, and he's going to be pissed, but I can't even force myself to care right now. This connection with Skyler is everything, and I don't want to resist it. I can't.

The only thing I'm second-guessing is if I was too rough on her. "You should have told me."

She presses her cheek against my chest. "I didn't want you to stop. I didn't want you to tell me that we should wait or that we shouldn't… you know."

I blow out a breath and brush my hand down her hair. "Baby, I would have waited until you were ready… I could have given you more time, made sure you were ready."

She leans her head back and looks at me. "More

ready than that? Is that even possible? I wanted you, Zach. Please don't regret what happened."

I cup her cheek. "Baby, there are no regrets."

I swear it's on the tip of my tongue to tell her I love her. I'm about to say it, but I hold back. When I tell her, I want to be able to do it with nothing hanging over our heads. No stalker, no pissed-off brother and friend. I want her to not have any reason to hold back from me.

"Are you okay?" I ask her.

She nods and blushes prettily.

I stroke a finger along her cheek. "Next time will be better."

She blinks in surprise. "Next time?"

I kiss her softly and pull back before it gets out of hand. "Yeah, baby. I told you that this is more than just a way to pass time. We're going to be together, Sky."

She opens her mouth but quickly closes it and leans into me, hiding her face. I want to ask her what she's thinking, but I feel that I've already pushed her limits, and we have time to figure out everything.

"Shower with me."

She's drawing circles on my chest, but at that, she stops. "You want me to shower with you?"

I nod. "Yeah, baby. Let's shower together."

I sit, drawing her up with me. My arms are around her, and I'm walking her to the bathroom when my phone rings. I look at it on the nightstand and tense. "It's Logan."

Sky's eyes widen, and I force a smile to my face. "Go ahead and get started. I'll be right there."

She moves to the bathroom but stands in the doorway, watching me. I pick up my phone and answer. "Hey, Logan."

There's static over the line, but I'm able to make out that he's asking about Sky. "She's fine. She had a brand trip, and we're up in Booker, TN."

Logan blurts out questions one after another. "Have you found the stalker? Where is Sky now? It's been days, Zach. Are you any closer to—"

Sky is staring at me from across the room, still naked. I have to avert my eyes from her body, so I stare up at the ceiling. "I'm getting close. There's been a few clues he's left. He had flowers delivered, and I was able to track down a description of the buyer from the florist."

Sky's mouth drops open. I've tried to shield her from the case as much as possible, and she's surprised that we have clues and are closing in.

"Where is my sister now?"

I let my gaze travel down Skyler's body. "She's here… in the hotel room."

Logan clears his throat. "You're sharing a hotel room?"

I grit my teeth. "I told you I'm not letting her out of my sight."

"Fuck," Logan curses. "So help me, Zach, she's my little sister."

I stand up and rub my hand across my face. "I know she's your sister." I suck in a breath and let it out. "We need to talk when you get back."

Skyler stands taller, surprise lifting her eyes.

"Zach," Logan says, voice strained. "I don't like the sound of that."

I hold my phone tighter. I don't want to have this conversation now, but I also don't want to hide from it. "You know me, Lo. You know who I am, and you know that I would never hurt Skyler."

"Mother fuckin' asshole. So help me, I will whoop your ass when I see you. Let me talk to my sister."

I cross my arms over my chest. "You want to talk to her, you need to calm down first. I won't have you upsetting her."

Logan gasps into the phone. "What the fuck? She's my sister."

I stand up and pace the floor. "She may be, but I'm still not going to let you upset her."

Skyler is wrapping a towel around her body as she walks over to me and holds her hand out. I want to protect her, but I remind myself that it's her brother, and she's been worried about him all week. I hand the phone over to her, and all I can hear is her side of the conversation.

"Hey, bub."

"Yes, I'm okay."

"I promise you, I'm okay."

"Yes, the brand trip is going good. When will you be home?"

"I love you too."

She hands the phone back to me, and I put it to my ear as I hold her with my free hand. I'm still naked, but she's covered her body with a towel, and I can't wait to peel it off of her. "Hey, Logan, how's the mission going? You need anything?"

He blows out a breath, and I can hear the frustration in his voice. "No, it's moving. Not as fast as I'd like, but it's okay. Take care of my sister, all right, brother?"

I tug Sky against my chest. "Yeah, I got her, Lo. Don't worry about anything here. Take care of yourself."

He grunts. "Yeah, and we'll have that talk when I get back."

He hangs up before I can answer him, and I toss my phone onto the bed. I pull at the towel wrapped around Sky's body. "Now how about that shower?"

She loops her arms around my neck, pressing her body to mine. "Okay."

I lift her into my arms, and she giggles. Right here and now, I know that I want to spend the rest of my life listening to her laugh.

CHAPTER 12
SKYLER

The morning after.

I've read about these and seen it talked about in television shows. I lie plastered to Zach's chest with his arms and legs wrapped around me. I don't want this to be awkward and know I should play it cool, but I'm not sure how to do that exactly.

Zach's voice is husky and sleep-laden. "What are you thinking about, Sky?"

I tense for just a second and then go limp in his arms. "The morning after. I'm not sure how this works. Do I act like last night was no big deal and just go about my day? Am I supposed to put my guard back up and try to get some distance between us?"

Instantly, his arms tighten around me. "Fuck that," he grunts.

I press my cheek against his bare chest. "Okay, fine. Then tell me how I'm supposed to act after last night."

He kisses the top of my head. "I don't want you to act any way. I want you to just be yourself."

I blink. "Okay, but I want you to know that just because it was my first time, I'm not going to turn into some clingy psychopath or anything. I know what last night was and—"

I'm flipped to my back, and Zach hovers over me. "Oh yeah, what was it?" He glares at me. "And if you say it was a one-night stand or some crazy shit like that, then I'm going to have to show you different."

My eyebrows shoot up. A part of me wants to mess with him just to see what he'll do, but another part of me doesn't want to play any games. I bury my face into his chest. "Well, I know what last night meant to me, but—"

He leans back, lifts my face, and gazes into my eyes. "What did it mean to you?"

I'm taken aback just looking at him. He's so handsome it's a little overwhelming. He was nicknamed Hollywood, Fabio, Handsome, and Hottie when he was younger, and none of them do him justice. He's just breathtaking to look at and way out of my league. I start to ramble. "Do you know how handsome you are?" Before he can answer, I shrug. "I mean, I'm sure you know, and honestly, it's a little overwhelming how beautiful you are."

"Sky—" He starts, but I don't let him interrupt me.

"Let me finish. So yeah, you're handsome and all the things, but to me, you've always been more than that. You probably don't remember this, but when I was ten, my parents made Logan take me to the park. I was playing by myself most of the time. You had met up with him there, and a bunch of you guys were playing basketball. Anyway, some kids were making fun of me. You stood in front of me, shielding me, and told them to back off. From that point on, I've always felt a connection with you."

I giggle awkwardly. "Gah, I'm telling myself to keep this light and then admitting to you that I've had a crush on you since I was a child." I try to pull from his arms. "Obviously, I'm not good at the morning after stuff."

I try to get up, but he rolls me over and uses his body to hold me to the bed. "My turn," he announces. "Do you know how beautiful you are, Sky?"

I roll my eyes, but he leans down, looking at me with so much intensity that I can't do anything but listen. "You're beautiful, smart, sexy, sweet. You're all the things. And when I look at you, I want things that I've never wanted before. I want to protect you… I want to be the one you turn to when you need something… Fuck, Sky, there are so many things I want when I'm with you that I don't know where to start."

There's a faint catch in my breath. "Me too."

He leans his head down to mine. "And there are things I want to say to you, but when I do, I don't want there to be anything holding us back. No stalker, no family uprising, nothing. So when this is over, we're going to talk, and we're going to make plans."

Hope flares in my chest. I smile widely at him. "I like the sound of that." I put my hands on his neck. "So now can I do something? Something I've been wanting to do?"

He nods. "Anything."

I smirk at him. "All right, remember that you said that."

I push him to his back, and he goes easily. I kiss his chest, right over his heart, and then I start to make my way down his taut stomach.

He sucks in a breath. "Sky… you don't—"

I cut him off. "I don't have to? Oh, I know that. I want to."

He trembles. Zach Campbell, who's a fierce protector and incredibly handsome, who can have any girl he wants, just trembled under my touch. When he says he wants me, I can't help but believe him.

I scoot down the length of him, and his manhood is already hard and proud, standing straight up. I sit between his legs and tentatively wrap a hand around it. I feather my finger along his length, and when I get to the tip, there's a glistening drop of precum. I run the pad of my finger around it and then lift it to my mouth, tasting his desire.

He groans, watching me through hooded eyes.

I pull my finger from my mouth. "I don't want to do this wrong."

He shakes his head. "You can't do anything wrong, Sky. Not with me."

I lean forward, kissing the tip of his cock. He moans, and that's all I need to bring me in further. I open my mouth and lick him from root to tip. His hands come up to cup my shoulders, and his whole body goes taut. I open my mouth, take him in, and don't stop until he hits the back of my throat. I swallow, trying to take him deeper, and the guttural groan that comes from his chest fills the room.

Slowly, I start to bob up and down.

"Look at me, Sky. I want your eyes on me."

I lift my gaze to his, and I'm surprised to see that his eyes are molten. Watching him, knowing that it's because of me that he's feeling pleasure is a good feeling. I take him deeper, moan around his girth, and get lost in the act of making him feel good.

But just as I feel him expanding in my mouth, he pulls me by the arms until I'm seated on his abdomen and his hard manhood is straight up, pressed against my ass. I try to catch my breath as he reaches between my thighs, coating his finger with my arousal. "Are you hurting?"

I shake my head, confused, trying to catch up.

He nods. "Ride me."

I bite my lip and look behind me then at his face again. Unsure, I ask him, "You want me to ride you?"

He nods, smiling ear to ear. "Fuck yeah, I do."

He helps me up, aligning his cock to my entrance. His hands grip my hips, holding me over him. I suck in a breath as I start to sink down.

Pleasure fills his face. I go slowly, committing it all to memory. The sensations, the sounds he makes, the way he makes me feel. It's only when I'm fully seated and can catch my breath that I start to move. I rotate my hips, front to back, side to side, and then up and down. It's when I'm riding him, grinding my clit into his pelvis that I start to move faster. We fall into a rhythm, and I feel him everywhere. He leans up, sucking a nipple into his mouth, coaching me on, telling me how beautiful I am and how he's never going to let me go.

The orgasm hits me, and it's like nothing I've ever felt before. He cups my face, forcing me to look at him, and as we both go over the cliff, staring into each other's eyes, I've never felt as connected to someone as I do in this moment.

I ride out the climax, grunting and groaning, and when I'm thoroughly exhausted, I lean over Zach, trying to catch my breath.

He pulls my hair off my face and holds me to him. "We're going to be late, and I'm not going to let you miss it."

I snuggle into him. "I could stay like this all day."

He groans. "Fuck, that sounds good, but it's not happening. Your favorite baker is doing a show today. We can do more of this afterward."

I lean up to look at him. "You're not bored with all this?"

He shakes his head, and I see the sincerity in his eyes. "Nope. Fuck, baby, just watching you is exciting for me."

I laugh and roll off of him and then look at the clock. "Oh… we have twenty minutes."

I'm about to get up, but he follows closely behind me, pulling me back against his chest. "We'll shower together so it will be faster."

I giggle. "You want to shower together to save time?"

He squeezes me to him as we walk to the bathroom. "I promise. I'll be on my best behavior."

I turn in his arms. "What if I don't want you on your best behavior?"

He turns on the water. "I won't let you miss it, Sky. But after… after… We can pick up where we left off."

As I stand under the spray of the shower, I let flashbacks from last night and this morning fill my head. There's so much I need to process, but for now, I'm just going to live in the moment.

CHAPTER 13
ZACH

Tense, I sit at Skyler's kitchen table. She's taping a segment for her ClipClap channel, and I would probably get more done if I worked from the other room, but I don't want to let her out of my sight.

This weekend was amazing. Being with Skyler, seeing her in her element, and getting to know her just affirms what I knew when I first saw her. She's going to be mine. Hell, she already is. I should probably have some regrets, but I don't have one. I look over at Skyler, watching her in her element as she glows talking about chocolate lava cakes and their gooey molten center. Fuck, nothing she says is sexual, but here I sit with a hard-on. Just being in the same room as her does that to me.

I force my eyes back to Skyler's laptop. Bakersking has been pretty quiet, and that should make me happy, but it actually puts me on edge. He's up to something. I can feel it in my gut, and my gut is never wrong.

I close Skyler's laptop and open mine to check my emails. My to-do list is ever growing. I have an interview for a receptionist. And I am supposed to meet with a prospective new client tonight. I send an email to Alex and tell him I need him at Skyler's house. Even though bakersking is being quiet, there's no way I'm leaving her unprotected.

After going through a few other emails, I close my laptop and then focus on Skyler as she finishes making her chocolate lava cake.

She's smiling ear to ear when she turns off her camera. There's dishes in the sink and on the counter. I bypass them and stop in front of Skyler, who is holding up a chocolate lava cupcake to me.

She tilts her head to the side. "I saw you looking. Want one?"

I'm staring into her bright blue eyes. "I was looking at you."

I lift my finger and point at her lip. "You have a little something… right here."

I'm about to wipe it off with my finger, but at the last second, I lower my hand and use my mouth instead, nibbling at the chocolate on her lips.

She melts into me, and I pick her up, setting her on the counter. Her legs widen, letting me lean between her thighs as I consume her lips in a kiss.

I'm about to suggest we go upstairs when the doorbell rings. Skyler pulls back, and it pains me to see that there is fear on her face. I brush her hair off her brow. "I hope it's okay. I need to interview a receptionist, and I had her come here."

Her eyebrows lift, and she laughs. "Sure, sure, nothing like inviting another woman to your girl… I mean… You know what I mean."

"My girlfriend's house," I finish for her, and she lights up. "Yes, I invited a woman here for an interview, but you should know by now that I'm not going to be looking at any woman other than you." I lean in and kiss her forehead. "And if you don't know that, then I'm fucking this up royally, and I'm going to fix it as soon as my interview is over."

The doorbell rings again. Skyler pushes against my chest, and as I step back, she jumps down. "Go, let's go meet her, and then I'll let you get on with it."

I laugh as I put an arm around her shoulder. "You want to meet her?"

She rolls her eyes. "This is Whiskey Run. I most likely know her."

Whiskey Run has been my home base forever, but I haven't spent a lot of time here, and that's something that I forgot. Everyone knows everyone—and everything—in this small town.

When we get to the door, I peek through the peephole, and when I see the woman on the other side, I realize I probably should have warned Skyler.

I disable the alarm, open the door, and stand back.

There's no hiding the surprise on Skyler's face. She's stunned and instantly opens her arms. "Bree! You're here! Oh my gosh, I haven't seen you… well, uh, in a long time."

I watch the two women hug, and it isn't the first time that I wonder if I'm doing the right thing.

As soon as Skyler releases Bree, she looks at me questioningly and then back to Bree. "Uh, are you applying for the receptionist job at Stronghold?"

Bree bites her lip. "Yes."

She pauses, waiting to see Skyler's reaction.

Skyler turns to me. "Uh, does Logan know about this?"

I cross my arms over my chest and shake my head. "No. I haven't mentioned it."

Sky inhales deeply and nods her head. "Okay. Okay."

She doesn't know what to say, and it makes me wonder what she knows about Bree and Logan. Sky hugs Bree again. "Well, I'm going to clean up the kitchen and let you all get to it."

I point to the living room. "Have a seat, Bree. I'll be right there."

She walks into the living room, and I put my hand at Skyler's lower back and lead her back into the kitchen. "Leave the dishes. I'll do them after I'm done with the interview."

She leans against the counter and smiles up at me.

"What if I have other plans for you after the interview?"

I groan and readjust myself. "Fuck, Sky, you're killing me here."

She just smirks at me.

I nod my head to the other room. "You think I'm fucking up by hiring her?"

Sky crosses her arms over her chest, tilts her head, and gives me a measured look. "Well, you've been friends with Logan for most of his life, so I think you know about his history with Bree."

It's not really a question, but I nod. "I do."

She lifts her chin. "So you know he needs to get his head out of his ass."

I smirk and point at her. "I know he deserves to be happy."

Her eyebrows lift. "And you think Bree will do that?"

For the first time, I'm questioning this. I ran into Bree when I first retired from Walker's Ghost Team. This idea has bloomed in my head until I can't get it out. I know Logan is going to be mad at me, but hopefully he can come to terms with it and see I'm doing it for his own good. "I hope that's the case. If nothing else, he needs closure."

Smiling, she taps a finger against my chest. "You're a good man, Zach Campbell."

I lean down and press a quick kiss to her lips. "I'll be back."

I'm almost to the door of the kitchen when I remember the other thing. "Oh yeah, I have a meeting with a prospective client tonight. I'm going to get Alex to come over while I'm gone."

She nods. "Okay. I'm going to The Whistler with Aria tonight."

"Skyler."

"Zach." She matches my tone. "What? It was on my calendar. My sister-in-law and I get together twice a month, and tonight is one of those nights."

I take a step toward her. "You have a stalker—"

She shakes her head. "And I'm not going to stop living my life because of him. I'm going tonight, Zach. Alex can go with me."

I growl. I don't know why. I trust Alex, and I know he would keep her safe, but it's not his job. I want to be the one to keep her safe. I want to be the one to go out with her.

I shift my weight side to side as I rethink the night. "Fine. I'll meet the client at The Whistler, and Alex and I will both be there."

She puts her hand at my waist. "Whatever you wanna do, Zach."

I quirk an eyebrow at her. "That was too easy."

She starts walking backward away from me. "What? You think I'm going to complain that you want to be with me? Because I'm not."

I put a hand to my chest, right over my heart and rub. She makes my heart race. I want nothing more than to take her upstairs to her bedroom and spend the rest of the afternoon there, but I have responsibilities and things I need to do.

One being the interviewee waiting for me in the other room. "I'll be back," I tell Skyler, and with one last longing look, I point to the back door. "Keep that locked."

She salutes me. "Aye, aye, Captain."

I smirk and shake my head. "Please keep that locked."

She practically preens, smiling at me. "You got it."

I force myself to walk away. As soon as I get to the living room and apologize to Bree for making her wait, she asks, "So Logan doesn't know I'm applying for the job?"

I shake my head. "No. Is that a problem?"

She nods. "Yeah, because he's most likely not going to like it, and we're probably just wasting each other's time." She shakes her head. "This is a bad idea."

I ignore her and pick up the resume and application that I printed out earlier. "You have the experience. Your background checks are clean, your job references are impeccable, and—"

She shakes her head with a look of defeat on her face. "None of that matters if Logan is going to come back into town and fire me on the spot."

I nod. "You're right. Which is why I would sign a contract that you will have a job for six months and then there will be an evaluation." Fuck, I hope I'm doing the right thing. "So you would have six months to prove yourself."

She tilts her head and seems to think about it. "And Logan couldn't fire me in those six months?"

"The contract would guarantee a job for six months." I hold my hands up. "Now, I don't pretend to know everything about you and Logan's situation but I would imagine when Logan gets back… well, he's not going to make it easy for you."

She lifts her chin. "One year."

I open my mouth, but before I can get anything out, she continues, "Make it that I'm guaranteed a job for one year and I'll do it."

I lift my hand and stroke it through the stubble of my chin. My instinct is to say yes. Logan needs this, whether he knows it or not. As I'm thinking about it, Bree continues. "You need help starting up your business, and I have experience doing that. I can put in all the systems, prepare training manuals, even train my replacement if it comes to that."

Fuck, I hope he forgives me for this. "Fine, you're hired. Can you start tomorrow?"

She nods. "Yes. I'll have a contract drawn up for you to sign."

I nod, and we talk about pay, hours, and other details of the job. When the interview is over, I walk her out to her car and meet Alex in the driveway.

Frustrated doesn't even begin to cover it. I'd hoped to have a little time with Skyler. "You're early."

He just laughs, not taking any offense. "That new client called the office and asked to move up the meeting, so I figured I'd better get here early so you could show me around."

I nod and I remind myself that after this is all over with, we'll have plenty of time alone together.

CHAPTER 14
SKYLER

"How are you holding up?" Aria asks me.

I look across the room where Zach is sitting with some buxom blonde, and I'm imagining pulling out every strand of her extensions and popping her inflated bust with a pin. "Fine," I answer shortly.

Aria follows my gaze, raises her eyebrows, and then looks back at me. "What's going on with the boyfriend over there?"

I gesture with my hand toward them. "Prospective client. Or so he says."

Aria waves her hand in front of my face. "Sky, you have to see how that man looks at you. You have nothing to worry about."

I shrug. "Yeah, right. Well, it doesn't matter. Who knows if this is real? I mean, he says it is, but what's that called when there are high stake situations and you fall in love—"

"Love!" Aria exclaims. "You love him?" She shakes her head. "I mean, I've heard about the crush you had when you were younger and how you told everyone that you were going to marry him one day, but love… that's just wow."

I scrunch my nose up. "Can we talk about something else?"

She leans toward me. "Seriously. How are you holding up with the whole stalker situation?"

I laugh and point at Alex, who is sitting at the next table. He's looking around acting like he's not listening to every word I say, but I know better. "Are you kidding me? That stalker doesn't have a chance. Zach has been with me every second. Except for tonight and he had Alex come follow me around."

I lean toward Alex. "No offense."

He just smirks without looking at me. "None taken."

I roll my eyes. "I mean, it sucks, it really does. Zach

says the guy is escalating, and that scares me, but I'm just trying to go about my business."

I look at my sister-in-law and notice the tiredness in her eyes for the first time. I'm so sick of focusing on me and my problems. "So how are you?" I ask her.

She gives me one of her fake smiles. "I mean, I'm good. You know… I'm fine."

I tilt my head and search her eyes. Aria and my brother Penn met at the hospital when she had just graduated physical therapy school and he was a brand new attending and they had the same patient. They fell in love and have been married around seven years now, but I've noticed a difference in them both recently, and I hate it because neither one of them is talking.

I lean toward her. "Aria… talk to me."

She looks as if she's about to burst into tears, and it scares the hell out of me. Aria is one of the strongest women I know. I grit my teeth. "What has my brother done?"

She wipes at one lone tear that has escaped her sad eyes and is rolling down her cheek. "Nothing. He hasn't done anything—"

I cut her off. "Don't defend him, Aria. You're obviously upset. What's wrong?"

She sucks in a breath and lets it out slowly. "Nothing. He works insane hours at the hospital. He's always on call and working on cases when he is home. It's just, I don't know, we're not connecting. Nothing's happened or anything."

I let out a sigh of relief. "Good, I thought you were going to tell me he cheated or something, and I was going to have to disown him."

Her mouth falls open as she stares at me. "Oh God, you think… he wouldn't cheat on me… would he?"

I realize my mistake, but there's no taking it back. "What? No. God, of course not. I'm sorry, I freaked out when you started crying. Penn would not cheat on you. He loves you."

She sniffs. "Yeah, he did. I mean… I don't know anymore."

I grab her hand. "Sis, talk to him. I know he's busy and all that, but he needs to make time for this. He has to because if he wakes up one day and it's too late and he can't fix this, then he won't survive it." I shake my head. "I'm telling you that man loves you… Why don't you plan a vacation or something? You need this… you both do."

Aria wipes at another tear. "He can't get away from the hospital. You know what? How about another drink? You want another one?"

She waves at the waitress, and when she comes over, Aria orders a Miami Vice and then gestures to me.

"I'll have a Miami Vice too."

The Whiskey Whistler is picking up. A lot of people come here after work to drink or just let off steam. Tonight there is a live band, and they're setting up, telling me that it's about to get loud and packed in here.

The waitress brings our drinks, and Aria takes a huge gulp. I wish I had the magic words to fix this, but I'm not sure what to say. One thing is for sure: My brother loves her. I have no doubt about that. As the youngest sister, my brothers don't look at me as their equal with my own thoughts and my own ideas. No, they have always looked at me as the one they have to protect, and when I was younger, just put up with. Penn wouldn't want to talk to me about this.

I say the only thing I can think of. "I'm so sorry, Aria. I really am, but I'm sure if Penn knew how you were feeling, he would fix this."

She opens her mouth to say something but quickly closes it. She throws up a hand and wipes her eyes again. "Look at us. We're supposed to be having fun here. Let's drink, let's talk about your new relationship, and then let's dance."

I know she's upset and just trying to get the topic of conversation off her. It has to be hard for her since I am Penn's sister. I nod. "Okay, it's a deal."

We look around the bar, and I find myself looking at Zach again. The woman has moved next to him instead of across from him, and she's relentless. In the span of one minute, she's touched him on the arm at least ten times and tossed her hair three times, and she's openly flirting with him like he belongs to her.

I grit my teeth and look back at Aria. "Let's dance."

She smiles and stands up, holding her hand out to me. As I stand up, I point at our drinks. "We should probably finish these. We don't want to leave them unattended."

Aria giggles, and as we stand across from each other, we finish off our drinks. We both set our empty glasses down and then walk out to the dance floor.

I stop next to Alex on the way. "We're going to dance."

He's already following us, looking between Zach and me.

I can see he's unsure what to do here, and so help me if he tells me I can't dance, I'm going to lose it on him.

But Alex just follows us, standing a few feet away with his arms crossed over his chest. I tune him out, along with Zach. I mean, if he wants the blonde's hands all over him, that's his prerogative, but I'm not going to sit and watch.

The next song is a line dance, and Aria and I line up. I get lost in the music and the movements. It's not until the end of the song that I see that Zach has moved into Alex's spot, and Alex is over at the booth with the blonde. Zach is watching me closely, nostrils flared, eyes dark. And I ignore him.

In reality, he didn't do anything wrong, but jealousy is an ugly thing.

The song ends, and Aria and I are laughing, waiting for the next song to begin. Two men come toward us, but they don't even get a word out. Zach steps in front of them. "Move along."

Both men have to lean their heads back to look at him and must figure they don't have a chance because they both walk away.

I spend the rest of the night ignoring Zach until Aria says she's tired and has to be up early tomorrow for work.

"Come on, I'll take you home," I offer.

She points at me and laughs. "You can't drive either."

I put a thumb over my shoulder. "Alex or Zach will give you a ride home."

I want to rip my brother's ass because he should be here. He should be with his wife. I trip over my own feet, making me realize that I may be a little drunker than I thought. Before I fall on my face, an arm goes around my waist, and Zach pulls me up against his chest. "Easy now. You okay?"

I pull from his hold. I'm mad at him, and maybe I'm being ridiculous, but I don't care. I point over my shoulder. "Don't you have a date waiting on you or something? I'm ready to go, and we need to take Aria home. Can you tell Alex?" I avoid looking at Zach. "Or I can get an Uber or something."

Zach puts a hand at the middle of my back. "Come on. I'll take you home." He looks at Aria. "You ready?"

She seems to find all this funny and laughs. "If you two want to be alone, I can find a ride."

I loop my arm through hers. "Don't be silly."

Zach walks us through the bar, and it makes me mad that every woman we pass is checking him out. I know he's a good-looking man, but I'm not ready for this crash of emotions to come over me. When we get outside, he points to his truck. "I'm right there."

He opens the back door, and I let Aria climb in before I get in after her. Zach doesn't seem bothered by us both riding in the back. I expect him to shut the door, but he surprises me when he leans in and pulls the seatbelt around me and snaps the lock.

He's looking all around as he walks to the driver's side, and Aria is elbowing me in the side with a little giggle. "That's so hot."

I look at her, surprised, and she holds her hands up. "Whoa there, tiger. I meant it's hot how Zach put your seatbelt on you. He wants you safe."

I shrug like it's no big deal, but on the inside, my lower belly pulls. Why am I being this way? It's not Zach's fault that he's so handsome and everywhere we go, women are looking at him.

Grudgingly, I ask Zach, "Do you know where Penn and Aria live?"

He looks at me in the rearview mirror. "I do."

I jerk my gaze from his and look out the window.

Aria elbows me in the side. She leans in to whisper in my ear, "Girl, he's got it bad. I would love if Penn looked at me the way Zach looks at you."

I look at my sister-in-law and see the pain on her face. I hate that she's not happy, and it makes me want to kick my brother's butt all over again.

On the way to Aria's house, we talk and laugh. When a popular song comes on the radio, I ask Zach to turn it up, and Aria and I sing along, laughing over our out of tune antics.

We're both smiling as Zach pulls into Penn and Aria's driveway.

When Zach parks, he gets out and hangs back by his truck as I walk Aria to her door. The lights are all out, telling me that my brother isn't home yet. I hate leaving her, knowing she's upset. "Want me to stay for a while?"

She pulls me in for a hug. "No, I'm fine. I love you, sis. Talk to you soon, okay?"

I nod, wishing I knew what to say to make things better, but I don't have a clue where to start.

I wait until she walks in the door, and when I turn, Zach is standing behind me. He holds his hand out, and I grimace before walking past him.

He jogs to catch up, opening the passenger side of the truck, and I reluctantly get in. He goes through the same steps, fastening my seatbelt and then closing my door and walking around to the driver's side.

I lean my head back on the head rest and close my eyes, hoping that Zach doesn't try to talk on the way home. I need some time to process everything.

CHAPTER 15
ZACH

Skyler acted as if she was sleeping the whole way home. It wasn't until I pulled into the garage that she opened her eyes and quickly got out.

I made sure everything was locked up and the alarm was reset before following her upstairs. I'm leaning against her open door while she's in the bathroom with the door closed. It's minutes later before she comes out. Her hair is in a knot on top of her head, her makeup is gone, and she's in a long T-shirt. I avert my eyes from her bare legs as she climbs into bed.

"Are you going to talk to me?"

She lies back on the pillow and stares at the ceiling. "What do you want to talk about?"

I move toward her. "Why are you mad at me? What did I do?"

She fires a look at me, and I swear I can feel the heat from it. "Really? You're going to ask me that?"

I stand beside the bed, hovering over her. "Yes, because I have no idea why you're so pissed."

She ignores me, and I walk around to the other side of the bed and start removing my clothes. She sits up then. "What are you doing? I'm mad at you… Go to the guestroom."

I chuckle, and her glare sharpens. "Sweetheart, I'm addicted to sleeping with you in my arms, so yeah, I'm not going anywhere."

Her mouth drops open, but she quickly closes it and shakes her head. "You can't sleep here. Why don't you see if the blonde from earlier wants you in her bed? I'm sure she does." She starts to mumble as she crosses her arms over her chest and lies down. "Prospective client, my ass. I didn't know you let all your clients touch you and—"

I lie down next to her and rest my head on my hand, looking at her. "Is that what this is about?"

She glares at me and then looks back to the ceiling.

I reach over and run my finger along her shoulder. "I think it's cute you're jealous."

Her mouth falls open, and she juts her chin. "Are you kidding me right now? I'm not jealous. All I'm saying is that you made it sound like there's something between us, and then the first blonde with big boobs that hits on you turns your head."

In full frustration, I move over her, holding her hands over her head against the bed. She struggles and then finally stops. She closes her eyes, but that's not going to work for me. "Look at me," I demand.

Her jaw tightens, and she glares up at me. "What?"

"She was a prospective client, and if you were paying attention, you would have realized that when I found out it was a personal bodyguard with benefits she was looking for, I told her we wouldn't be taking the job... and I told her that I was in a serious relationship with you."

She blinks at me. "You did not."

It's my turn to roll my eyes. "Sky, I showed her pictures of you on my phone, told her you were going to be my wife one day, and then left her with Alex to make sure she got home okay."

Skyler's chest rises and falls rapidly. "You... you didn't say that."

I lean down until we're nose to nose. "I've tried telling you that this is serious between us. Maybe you should start listening to me."

She exhales, her face open and unguarded. "Zach... look at you... you're always going to have women hitting on you."

I don't even hesitate. "I don't want them. It's you I want to be with." I clear my throat. "I know this is fast. I know you have a lot going on, but I need you to believe in us, Sky. I need you to let me love you."

She shrugs, and her voice is small as she says, "I'm scared."

I bring one of her hands up and put it at my chest, right over my heart. It's beating rapidly as if it's about to come right out of my chest. "Me too. I'm scared I'm going to let you down. I'm scared you're going to come to your senses and know you can do better than me. I'm scared that after all is said and done, you're going to know that I'm the last person you should choose."

She drags her hand from my chest to cup my cheek. "I love you, Zach. There's a part of me that has loved you since I was just a kid. But this, what I'm feeling now, is so much bigger… so much more than I've ever felt before."

I nod, because I know exactly what she means. "Me too."

She loops her arms around my neck and pulls me down so that our bodies are flush against each other. She holds me to her, and I revel in being in her arms.

I lift my head and look into her eyes. "You know, you're not the only one that is jealous."

She playfully smacks my chest. "I wouldn't call it jealous."

I chuckle and roll to my side, pulling her with me. "Okay, well, I'll straight-up tell you, I was jealous."

She gasps like she doesn't believe me. "Jealous? What do you have to be jealous about? There wasn't some man touching me."

I grit my teeth, thinking about her on the floor out there, dancing and laughing. She's so fuckin' beautiful, and I wanted to kill every motherfucker that thought they had the right to look at her. "When you were dancing, I thought I was going to have to fight every man there. You're so beautiful,

Sky, that every man was watching you, wishing they could talk to you or touch you. The only thing that kept me out of jail was knowing I would be the one going home with you tonight."

Her smile takes over her whole face. "Well, I'm home now… so what are you going to do with me?"

She barely gets the challenge out of her lips than I'm reaching for her shirt, lifting it up her body. She's bare underneath, no panties or bra. I grunt, looking at her round breasts with plump nipples. "Fuck, if I'd known you were naked underneath here…"

My voice trails off as I circle her nipple with my finger. Her body arches, pushing her breast into my hand. I lean down and suck one nipple before moving to the other. I slide a hand down her body and cup her mound, sliding a finger through her swollen, wet slit.

She groans, and I raise up to look at her. "I want you."

She nods. "I want you too."

I sit up and take off my clothes and then position myself between her legs. "I need to be inside you, Sky, and I don't want to wait."

She answers me by letting her legs fall open. I look at her glistening cunt and gulp as I run a finger through her folds. "Tonight, while you were on that dance floor, men ogling you, wanting you, this is what calmed me. Knowing that this… that you… were mine."

She stretches her body. "Yes, I'm yours. You're the only one I want to see me like this, Zach."

I wrap my fist around my girth and line it up at her center. Slowly, I enter her, and after she adjusts to me, I start to move leisurely.

The friction is too good, and I know I won't last long. She fits me like a glove, and as I move in and out of her, more than ever, I want her eyes on me.

"Look at me, Sky."

She peels her eyes open. They're a dark shade of blue and hooded with arousal, but she looks at me.

As I move in and out, having her eyes on me makes it all even more intense. Emotions well inside me. This feels special and overwhelming and bigger than anything I've ever experienced before. "Fuck, you feel so good, baby."

She groans as she meets me thrust for thrust.

I lean over and kiss her lips. As I thrust deeper, the kiss gets more intense. I reach between us, strumming her clit, and she goes off like a rocket. Her body tenses, she whimpers against my lips, and her pussy clamps down on my dick. My orgasm is instant, and I take her deeper, wishing that she wasn't on the pill and that filling her up with my seed would tie her to me forever.

Soon. Soon, she will be mine in every sense of the word. Until then, I'm going to show her how much I want her, how much I need her, and how good we can be together.

CHAPTER 16
SKYLER

I step out of the bathroom, and Zach is lying naked on the bed, hands behind his head. I can't help but drink him in, every line, every flex of his muscles, the slow rise and fall of his chest. "Well, good morning."

He grunts, jerking his hips. "You're beautiful."

I laugh and tug at the knot on the top of my head. "I have no makeup on, my hair is a disaster, and—"

He sits up, the bed dipping where he moves. "You're beautiful. Do I need to show you just how beautiful I think you are?"

I hold my hand up and move across the room to the door. "As tempting as that is, I'm going to go make breakfast, and then I want to try out a new recipe for my live tonight."

That gets his attention, and he pats his stomach. "What is it?"

I cross my arms over my chest. "Do you really care? You eat everything I bake."

He laughs. "No. Whatever it is, I'm going to love it."

My heart does that ridiculous flip again. I'm still trying to process all of this. Being loved by Zach is a new feeling, but it's the best one. I've never had anyone as interested in my baking as he is. But it's not just baking; it's everything. He truly listens to me. He notices. He tastes my failed recipes and compliments me at every turn. I point to the door. "Are you coming down soon?"

He nods his head just as his phone buzzes on the nightstand. He looks at the caller ID, and I see the fast flash of guilt on his face. "It's your brother, Miller. I'll be right down." He stands up, and I watch as he pulls on his jeans before answering the phone.

I take my time walking down the stairs, but I'm smiling the whole way. I turn on the kitchen lights and look around my spotless kitchen. It's probably my favorite room in the house, which is good since I spend most of my time here. I unlock the back door for Terry and then go to get my pans out, setting them on the stove. I then go to the fridge and grab the carton of eggs, bacon, and apple butter. I'm juggling everything in my arms when I sense there's someone behind me.

I freeze. Instinct takes my breath as arms go around me. I know it's not Zach. The grip is not warm or safe. I don't recognize the smell of sweat, cigarettes, and body odor. I freeze for just a second, unsure what to do but knowing I need to do something.

I drop all the contents in my arms, but before I can get a scream out, a hand covers my mouth. Panic hits me, hot and fast.

The man jerks me back, holding me to him with one arm around my waist and the other hand over my mouth, covering my screams.

His grip tightens around me, and he's breathing into my ear. "I knew you'd smell like sugar cookies."

He leans down and licks my cheek.

Something inside me snaps. I swing, I bite, I kick, I elbow him hard in the ribs, but he doesn't loosen his hold. I fight him for everything I'm worth. I try tossing elbows, biting his hand, stomping and kicking at him, but no matter how hard I fight, I can't get free.

"Stop it," he grunts. "I don't want to hurt you, but I will."

And that's when I see it. A knife. My knife. He's using my knife from the holder on the kitchen counter against me. I feel the tip at my neck and freeze. I don't even take a breath. It's like everything around me magnifies: the hum of the refrigerator, Terry's knock on the back door, the unsteady beat of my heart. "Please," I muffle under his hand.

"Are you going to be quiet?"

I nod my head, and he uncovers my mouth.

I know I'm going to scream, but I can't do it with his knife at my throat. All I hear is a voice, and it's a weird feeling, being scared but also wanting to face my attacker head-on.

The fact that Zach is upstairs and knowing he'll be down soon comforts me a little. I just need to keep this guy talking.

"What do you want?" I ask him.

"You." He chuckles, lifting his hips to press into my backside.

I almost vomit. I have to swallow it back and keep it together. "Who are you?"

He buries his face in my hair and inhales. "I'm your Baker King."

Oh God. Zach said that bakersking was escalating, but I didn't really know what that meant. I thought this was someone that was all talk, and I never dreamed he would break into my house. "Please, I'm begging you—"

He cuts me off as he leans me over the counter. The hard surface digs into my hip as the man pulls the knife from my neck, but as soon as I start to struggle again, he puts it back. "Stop it. I don't want to hurt you, but I will."

"I don't think so," Zach says from the doorway.

He's still shirtless, jeans hanging low on his hips, but what surprises me most is the gun in his hand pointed right by my head at bakersking.

I shake my head. "I'm sorry. I unlocked the door."

Zach is watching the bakersking, but his voice is for me. "It's okay, honey. This isn't your fault."

Dang, I wish I could believe him. I'm the one that unlocked the door without even thinking about it. What was I even thinking? Obviously, I wasn't. As I have this mental talk with myself, Zach moves toward us.

Terry continues knocking from the back door, hollering my name, and my attacker gets even more agitated.

Bakersking jerks me to him even harder and bellows at Zach. "Stop! Don't come any closer or I'll cut her."

Zach's face distorts into anger. "You hurt her, and I'll kill you." His words are lethal and experienced.

His chest is rising up and down, and I can feel the anger coming off of him in waves. His face, usually void of any emotion, is filled with anger, pain, regret, guilt, and worry. I hate that I've put him in this position.

It's like I can see the flashbacks on his face. Things he's seen while serving, and he's experiencing it all again.

I don't know what to say or how to make this better,

so I say the one thing I want him to know in case this goes south really quickly.

"Zach."

He doesn't look at me. Even from across the room, I can see the pulse in his neck pumping. I say his name again. "Zach."

He finally looks at me, and I soften my gaze, wanting him to see the sincerity on my face. "I love you, Zach. No matter what, I love you."

"No!" bakersking screams. He loses it, jerking me back and forth, and then he raises his hand before punching me in the face. "You don't love him, you love me!"

The pain is excruciating, and as I'm falling to the ground, I hear a gunshot, and then everything goes black.

I'm not sure how long I'm out, but even though I can't open my eyes, I can hear everything.

Zach's hands are on me as he whispers to me, trying to reassure me.

Terry is here too, cursing, saying he'll call 911, and the panic in his voice worries me.

Am I dying?

I hear sirens and then more voices in the room.

A man calling out details. "Male patient. GSW to the right shoulder. Bleeding controlled and vitals are stable."

"Female patient, blunt force trauma to the face, possible concussion. Eyes closed but responds to verbal stimuli. Breathing spontaneous, airway intact, vitals stable."

I reach for Zach, and he puts his hand in mine. "Don't let me go. Please don't let me go."

I wait for him to reassure me. I want to hear his voice, but he's silent. The only thing he gives me is when he squeezes my hand.

I don't let myself fall back into the darkness until I hear him say, "I'm going to ride with her to the hospital."

CHAPTER 17
ZACH

I fucked up.

There's no other way to say it. I fucked up, and with my fuck-up, I almost got Skyler killed.

She's lying on the hospital bed. She's so pale, and she's been sleeping for so long, I can't help but be worried.

Penn has been in here multiple times to check on his sister, and every time he's walked in here, he's looked at me blankly. It's obvious he doesn't know whether to thank me that his sister is alive or tell me to get the fuck out since I let her get hurt.

I've replayed it over and over in my head. Seeing Skyler standing in the kitchen with that asshole's hands on her is something that I'll never forget. It's my fault he was able to get close to her. And fuck, he put his hands on her, he fuckin' hit her. Everything in me wanted to kill him. I should have.

I gently touch Skyler's hand, wishing she would wake up and I could see her blue orbs looking at me.

She deserves more than me. Seeing the bruise on her face makes me physically sick, but I can't look away.

I hear the commotion from the hallway, and I stand up as her brothers and sister-in-law pile into the room. Penn, Aria, Miller, Guy, and Ozzy all look at Skyler on the bed with worried expressions. They gather around her, all talking at once. I release my hold on her and back away from the bed, shame filling me. She's lying there hurt because of me. I should have done better. I shouldn't have let her out of my sight.

Overwhelmed, I walk out of the room and lean against the wall. I can hear them talking, and Penn explains her injuries. They all talk about taking turns sitting with her and taking care of her. I want to be the one with her, but I lost that right.

Miller comes out of the room, and he looks as if he's aged ten years. He's worried. Hell, we all are. "Hey," he says, looking at me curiously.

I nod, ready for him to hit me. I brace myself for it. I won't do anything to stop him because I deserve it.

"Thank you," he murmurs with pain in his voice.

I shake my head and put my head in my hands. "Fuck, don't thank me. I don't deserve thanks."

Miller points toward the room. "She's alive, Zach. That fucker could have… he could have…"

Miller can't even say the words. He's a hard-ass. He doesn't tiptoe around things, but he doesn't want to think about his little sister getting hurt.

I clench my eyes shut as the image of a blade at Skyler's neck flashes into my mind. I can't unsee it. Or how I walked in and he had her bent over the counter, pressing into her and the pure agony on her face. I let that happen. I let that man touch her.

I open my eyes, and Miller is looking at me like I'm a bomb about to go off. Hell, maybe I am. I can't just stand here and do nothing.

"Are you all going to be here with her?"

Miller looks toward the room and then back at me. "Yes, but... she'd want you here."

She would. I know she would, and that makes me feel even worse. I let her down, and she will still say this is not my fault. "I need to go to the police station. I need to make sure he's behind bars and isn't going anywhere."

Miller brings his phone out of his pocket. "I'll make a call, but I guarantee he won't go anywhere."

I start walking backward down the hall. The walls feel like they're closing in on me, and I have to get out of here. "Don't leave her by herself. I'll be back... I just need some air..."

I turn and practically run from the hospital. I don't stop until I'm outside, and then I bend over, sucking in a breath and trying not to pass out.

The world feels as if it's spinning, and I walk slowly to a tree and lean against it. I want to leave. I want to run from here as fast as I can, but I can't. I can't leave, knowing Skyler's here in the hospital.

I take a few deep breaths and then pull my phone from my pocket. I call Alex, and he answers on the first ring. "How's Skyler?"

"She's going to be okay," I tell him. She has to be okay. "Are you at the police department? I need to know he's behind bars."

"He is. And just so you know, this isn't his first time. He has a huge rap sheet. Stalking charges, rape, assault… the list goes on and on."

Fuck, I should have killed him.

Alex continues, unaware of my thoughts. "They're sending a badge over to you. They interviewed Terry here, but they wanna talk to you and Skyler."

I look toward the hospital. I can't let her face this alone. I start walking back. "Okay. Thanks for the heads up, Alex."

I walk through the hospital, the beeping machines and various voices filling my head. When I get to her room, I hesitate. I'm standing in the hall when I see the policeman walking toward me. I block his path from entering the room. "Let me make sure she's up for this, okay?"

He nods. "You're Zach Campbell, right?"

I nod, and he points at me. "I need to talk to you too."

I hold a hand up, telling him to stay right here, and then I walk back into Skyler's room. She's sitting up in the bed, surrounded by her brothers and sister-in-law.

Penn looks at me and then his sister. "Okay, well, I think we should let the patient rest."

I'm looking at Skyler and point a thumb over my shoulder. "The police are here and want a statement from you and me. Do you feel up to it? If not, I can send him away."

She waves her hand. "No, it's fine. You'll stay with me, right?"

I nod, but I'm unable to meet her eyes. She should hate me right now. Fuck, she shouldn't want me near her.

Each of her brothers hugs her and tells her they will be by to see her later. She points at Penn. "If you want to see me, I'll be at home. I'm ready to get out of here. Make it happen, Penn."

He nods. "Yeah, yeah, the nurse is working on discharge papers right now." He turns to me. "Will you make sure she gets home?"

My tongue feels thick, so I don't attempt to answer him, I just nod my head. He looks at me strangely and then ushers his brothers out of the room but not before each of them shake my hand, thanking me on the way out.

Aria hugs Sky. "You need anything, you call me, okay?"

She nods, hugging her sister-in-law tightly. Aria gives me a warning look as she walks by, and I'm not sure what to make of it. I still can't believe neither she nor the brothers have kicked my ass yet.

Sky says my name softly. "Zach."

I don't let her finish. I point toward the door. "I'm going to get the officer."

I don't wait for her to say anything. I bring in the cop, and he goes over to the bed.

"I guess you had a wild morning."

Ever patient and friendly Sky nods her head, smiling, even though it doesn't quite reach her eyes. "Yes, Officer."

He pulls out his pad of paper. "Okay, can you tell me about it?"

Skyler starts talking about how she went down to the kitchen and unlocked the back door because her assistant would be arriving soon. She says she was gathering items out of the fridge to make breakfast and the man come up behind her. She tells him everything: the knife to her neck, the ways he touched her, and then how I came into the room.

She's looking at me like I'm some kind of hero, and I can't stomach it. She talks about how scared she was and tells the police officer that when she said she loved me, the man hit her.

It guts me. Literally, she was beaten for loving me. I'm no good for her. Everything inside of me is telling me to run, but my feet are like lead glued to the ground.

The police officer looks at me. "Are you her boyfriend? Husband?"

I lift my chin. "I was hired to protect her."

His eyebrows skyrocket, and he gives me a dirty look. He can't make me feel any worse than I already do. "Right. Uh, okay. Then what?"

Skyler is staring at me as if she's trying to figure me out. Well, good luck with that because I can't even begin to explain everything I'm feeling right now. Skyler's soft smile disappears. "After I was hit, I blacked out, I guess. I don't know what happened after that."

The policeman looks at me. "Mr. Campbell?"

I cross my arms over my chest. "He uh, dropped the knife and hit her. I shot him, but it was too late. I ziptied his hands. Terry was at the back door. I guess the assailant locked the door behind him, so I let Terry in, told him to call 911, and then I tended to Skyler until the ambulance got there."

He's writing it all down. "And this guy, Leo Reynolds, has been stalking you?"

Before Skyler can answer, I tell him, "Yes, he's been stalking her. I have everything in his file that I'll send over to you."

He nods. "Your employee, uh, Alex Colby, gave it to us." He finishes writing and then closes his pad. "Okay, well, I think I have everything I need." He looks at Skyler. "Just so you know, Mr. Reynolds has a big rap sheet, and he's going to be in prison for a long time."

Skyler brings her knees up and wraps her arms around her legs. "Good. Can I leave now?"

At that moment, the nurse comes in. "Who's ready to get out of here?"

Skyler smiles. "Me! I am."

I walk the officer to the door while Skyler and the nurse go over the paperwork. She refuses the wheel chair, and in no time, we are walking out of the hospital. There's a thousand things I want to say to her, but I don't know where to start.

CHAPTER 18
SKYLER

He's not talking. He's not saying a word.

The Jasper hospital is thirty minutes from my house, and he doesn't open his mouth the whole way home. Instead of pulling into my garage, he parks in the driveway, and my stomach sinks. He's not staying.

I get out of his truck and walk up to the door. I don't have anything. No keys, nothing, but Terry opens my door for us. "Oh my God, you're okay!" He hugs me and puts an arm around my shoulder as he walks me into the house.

He sits me down on the couch. "Are you okay?"

I nod, peeking a look at Zach. He's leaning against

the wall, arms crossed, a blank expression on his face.

I mutter to Terry, "Yeah, I'm okay. A little bruised, but it could have been much worse."

Terry worriedly starts listing things. "I've scheduled some of your drafts for social because I figured you'd want to take a few days off."

"But—" I start.

Terry interrupts me. "Skyler, you need to give it a few days at least. You won't be able to hide those bruises behind makeup right now."

Reluctantly, I nod. I know he's right, and even though I can't go live or tape any new videos, I can bake. I have to bake; it's how I cope with things.

Terry continues, reminding me why I hired him. "I cleaned up the kitchen. I knew you wouldn't feel like cooking anything, so I made a meat, cheese, and fruit charcuterie board for you to snack on." He finally takes a breath. "Do you need anything else?" He looks at Zach, frowns, and then looks back at me. "I can hang around and help you or whatever."

I wait for Zach to say he's got it or that he's going to be here, but he says nothing. I shake my head.

"Thank you for everything today, Terry. You're the best. Why don't you take tomorrow off and we'll get back to our regular schedule—"

Terry sits down on the coffee table. "I'm so sorry, Sky. I feel horrible that he was able to get in because you unlocked the door for me."

I reach over and squeeze his arm. "Don't. None of this is on you. That guy is crazy."

He nods sadly before standing up. "Okay, well, I'm going to go and let you rest. Call me if you need anything. And Janie has been calling constantly, checking on you. We can come sit with you or, well, whatever you need."

I kick off my shoes and pull my legs up under me. "Thank you, Terry."

He stops next to Zach, says something under his breath, and then walks through the house. It's not until I hear the back door close that I lift my chin to Zach. "Are you okay?"

He jerks like I physically hit him or something. "God, don't ask me that."

I wrap my arms around my knees, holding my legs to my chest. "Talk to me, Zach. Are you mad at me? I told you that I'm sorry for unlocking the door."

He clenches his eyes shut and shakes his head. "Don't apologize to me. You have nothing to be sorry for."

I move to the edge of the couch and let my feet touch the floor. All these emotions are swirling inside me, but I force myself to stand up and move toward him. He tenses the closer I get. I stop when I'm standing right in front of him. I know he's got things he's trying to work through, but I'm not ashamed for what I'm about to ask him. "Zach."

He whispers, "Yeah?"

I lean my head back to look up at him. "I can't even pretend to know what you're feeling right now or what you're thinking, but I need something from you."

"What... what do you need?" His voice cracks on the last word.

"I want to sleep—"

He gives me a helpless look. "You can, but I'm going to have to monitor you through the night. Doctor's orders."

I tip my head and search his eyes. "You sure you want to do this? I can get Aria or one of my brothers over here."

He shakes his head firmly once. "I can do it."

I nod. "Okay. Well, what I need is to lie down and for you to hold me. Nothing else, just hold me."

He swallows hard. "I can do that."

I should let it go, but I stay right where I'm at. "Can you hug me, Zach? I just need…"

I don't know how to explain what I need, but after everything today, I feel like I'm losing touch with me, with him, with my whole damn life.

He hesitates, and my stomach sinks, but he finally brings his arms up and wraps them around me. He holds me so tightly I can barely take a breath, but I don't complain. I practically melt into him, wondering if he can absorb some of what I'm feeling.

He kisses the top of my head. "Come on. You have to be exhausted. Let's get you to bed."

I nod but don't move. I'm afraid if I let him go, this is it. He's been acting strangely since this morning, and I'm so afraid he's going to walk out that door and I'll never see him again. He picks me up, holding me to his chest.

I look up at him, but he's staring straight ahead.

He carries me upstairs and sets me on the end of the bed. He pulls the covers down and then helps me get comfortable. He's treating me like a child, but I happily go along with it. He starts to stand up, but I hold my hands out to him. "Lie down with me."

His eyes are filled with pain. "Sky, I don't think that's a good idea."

I know he's dealing with things. Hell, he shot someone today, and I know that can't be easy on him. I don't want to beg, but I'm not above it. "Please. I just want you to hold me."

He lies down next to me, on top of the covers. I press my body against his, and after a brief moment, he wraps me in his arms.

My cheek is pressed against his chest, and the steady thump of his heart beating is soothing in a way I can't explain. "Thank you."

He tenses under me, but I continue. "Thank you for today, Zach. If you weren't here… if you didn't show up when you did…"

His voice is raw. "Please, don't thank me. He should never have been able to touch you."

I clench my eyes shut, trying to not let my mind go there. "But it could have been so much worse."

His silence worries me. I want to ask him about it, but sleep starts to take me.

I'm not sure how long I've been asleep, but when I wake up, Zach is sitting on the chair in the corner of the room, just staring at me. I start to get up, and he's by my side in an instant. "What's wrong? What do you need?"

I laugh and throw the covers off. "I need to pee."

He scoops me up in his arms and carries me to the bathroom.

"Zach, I can walk."

He just grunts. He doesn't say anything else until he sets my feet on the bathroom floor and then hovers next to me. "Are you hungry? You didn't eat breakfast or lunch, and you should eat something."

"Yeah, I could eat."

He stands there, staring at me, and I give him a playful shove. "You, uh, going to go so I can take care of business?"

He doesn't smile. Doesn't laugh, nothing. He backs out of the bathroom and grabs the door, not closing it all the way. "I'll be right here if you need me."

I pull my pants down and sit, but even though I need to go, I can't. "Zach."

Instantly, he has the door open and is standing in front of me. I put a hand up. "Hey, uh, can you close the door? I can't do this with you listening to me."

He doesn't want to, but he walks back out and shuts the door. Quickly, I take care of my business, wash my hands, throw some water on my face, and then brush my teeth. My hair is standing up all over the place, so I pull a brush through my wayward strands.

Only when I feel more put-together do I walk back out of the bathroom. Zach is waiting for me, and he doesn't say anything, just scoops me up and carries me back to bed. "Lie down and I'll get you something to eat."

As soon as he releases me, he's practically sprinting from the room.

I put my back against the headboard and look at

the empty doorway. An uneasy feeling comes over me.

When Zach comes back, he's carrying a drink and a big plate of food. He sets the water bottle on the nightstand and holds the plate out to me. It's filled with crackers, meats, and cheeses. "This looks good."

"Terry," he explains.

I nod and take a bite. I pull my feet up under me. "Have a seat."

Instead of sitting on the bed next to me, he sits on the chair. I take a few bites, thinking of what I need to say, and when I think I have my thoughts together, I set the plate down on the empty bed beside me. "Talk to me."

Zach is staring at his hands. "What do you want to talk about?"

CHAPTER 19
ZACH

I knew that we were going to have this conversation, but I don't want to do it now. Skyler moves to the side of the bed, letting her legs dangle over the side so she's facing me. "What's going on? What's wrong?"

I stand up and start pacing the bedroom. "What's wrong? You could have been killed today. You could have been—"

She cuts me off. "But I wasn't."

I stop, facing the wall, unable to look at her. "But you could have been, Skyler. I fucked up. I shouldn't have—"

I stop, unable to say the words that I've been thinking all morning. So many scenarios have played out in my head. If I had kept my distance and treated this like the job it was, I would have been downstairs already. I wouldn't have been in her bedroom while she was down there being attacked.

I can hear the hurt in Skyler's voice. "You shouldn't have what?"

I open my mouth but quickly close it. I can't say it. I shake my head.

Hurt turns to anger. "No, Zach, you don't get to just stand there and say something like that and not finish it. What is it? What shouldn't you have done?"

I let my head hang. I fucked up, and I don't know how I can explain that to her.

Her voice is small and broken. "You shouldn't have had sex with me? Shouldn't have made me love you? Shouldn't have what, Zach?"

I turn, and she's right in front of me. Looking at her brings it all back. Hell, if I blink, I see it. The glint of the blade, the terror in her eyes, the way her head went back when he hit her. All of it is on a constant replay in my head. "This was a job, Skyler. I was hired to protect you… and I failed."

She backs away from me, trembling. "I was a job? That's all I was to you? I don't believe that. I was there and—"

I hold my hands up. "Sky, stop. Don't get upset. We can talk about this later."

She shakes her head, her eyes shining with unshed tears. "No, I don't want to talk about this later." She sucks in a deep breath. "Do you love me?"

That question is like a bullet to my chest. It hits me hard, and I have to hold back the truth that I want to shout to her. Of course I love her. I'm fucking consumed with it. I want to scream yes, but my throat closes around the word. She deserves more. "It doesn't matter if I love you or not. I'm no good for you, Sky."

Stricken, she jerks as if I've physically hit her. She puts her hand over her chest as if she's trying to hold her heart in place. "It doesn't matter if you love me?"

I take a step toward her. "Sky, listen…"

She puts her hands up. "So what is this, Zach? Are we over? Is that what you're saying?"

"I'm not leaving you until I know you're okay."

She laughs, and it sounds hysterical. "Okay? You're not leaving me until you know I'm okay? Are you even listening to yourself? I'm not going to be okay. The man I love, the man I thought I had a future with, doesn't want to be with me."

"Sky, please, you shouldn't get upset, you shouldn't—"

She cuts me off. "Get out."

I plant my feet on the floor. "I'm not leaving you like this."

She glares at me. "Get out, Zach. I want you out of my house."

She's so angry, and I can't say I blame her. More than anything I want to hold her to me and never let her go, but she deserves more. Since the moment I saw that guy holding the knife to her neck, I've been lost. I was on a mission. I went through the motions and neutralized the attacker, but this mission was like nothing I've ever felt before. It was the most important one to me, the most personal one, the one I couldn't fail at—and I did. I failed, and I did it royally.

I want to explain to her and make her understand

why we can't be together, but she's not going to listen. I have to try, though. "Sky, please."

She glowers at me. "Go, Zach. I don't want you here."

I put my head down and walk out of the room. The whole way down the stairs and to the front door, I want to stop and beg her to forgive me. I don't want to let her go, but I know that in the end, she's going to realize she deserves better than me. As soon as I get downstairs, I type in the code to set the alarm and then close and lock the door behind me. I sit on the stoop and call Aria, Penn's wife.

She answers tentatively. "Hello?"

"Aria, this is Zach. Uh, can you come over and stay with Skyler?"

"Sure, absolutely. Let me pack a bag and I'll be right there. Is she okay?"

I swallow. She'll be okay. She'll forget about me in no time. I'm the one that doesn't know if I'll survive this. "Yes, uh, she asked me to leave, but I don't want her to be here by herself."

Her silence is telling. "What did you do?"

I blow out a breath. "I didn't protect her."

More silence. "What? But she's okay… you saved her."

I practically choke out the words. "He had a knife to her throat. He almost…" I let my voice trail off. "Look, she's better off without me. She's not in danger anymore, but she needs to be monitored with her concussion, and she doesn't want me here. I'm just upsetting her."

I prepare myself for her to tell me off or to give me a piece of her mind. She does neither. "Yeah, okay, I'll be right there."

She hangs up, and I put my phone in my pocket. I stand up, pacing around the yard of Sky's house. I check the doors. I lock the gate to the backyard. I check the windows on the first level, and then I go back to the front yard to pace some more.

It doesn't take long for Aria to get here, and when she does, she looks at me curiously, shaking her head. "I don't know if I need to throat punch you or if I need to talk some sense into you."

She looks at me with hope, but I avoid her gaze. I'm barely holding it together. "It's better this way. She'll forget about me."

Aria opens her mouth and then closes it. She shakes her head and then puts her hand on her hip. "I know my sister-in-law, Zach, and she's not going to forget about you." She tips her chin at me. "But if you're just willing to let her go, then maybe she should."

Aria throws her bag over her shoulder and turns to walk into the house, but she stops only a few feet from me. "Zach, you think you failed her, but she thinks you saved her. Don't twist this into something it's not." She points to her head and then to her heart. "Don't let whatever you got going on up here mess with what's in here."

She doesn't get it. She doesn't know. I go to my truck and get in. I tell myself that I'm sitting here just to make sure Aria gets inside, but in truth, I'm hoping to get just one more glimpse of Skyler.

CHAPTER 20
SKYLER

I hit pause on the recording and walk over to sink into the chair at the kitchen table. I feel drained, but I'm doing my best to not act like it. It was a rough night last night. I tossed and turned for most of it, and I can easily blame it on the stalker, but that's only half of it. I miss Zach. I don't want to, and heck, I wish I could turn off whatever this is, but I can't.

Aria sips at her coffee, munching on the banana bread I made this morning. "If I stay here much longer, I'm going to be ten pounds heavier."

I laugh, trying to act as if my heart isn't breaking in two. My family is worried about me. I've heard from every brother except for Logan, but he's supposed to be getting back into town today.

"I'm sure Penn is missing you at home," I say lightly.

She shrugs but doesn't agree with me. I'm about to ask her again about what's going on with my bonehead brother, but I save my breath. She's tight-lipped about it, and no matter what I say or ask, she's not telling me. Hopefully, they'll work things out. They have to because if there's ever two people that love each other, it's them.

She smiles softly. "Are you tired of me already?"

I shake my head. "No, of course not. But I'm sure you are supposed to be at work or something, right?"

"I took a few days off."

I let my head fall back with a groan. "Ugh, I wish you hadn't done that. Listen, I'm okay. I promise you, I'm okay. Yeah, yesterday was scary, but it could have been so much worse."

She studies me over the rim of her mug. "Right, well, what about everything with Zach? How's that going?"

I scrunch my nose up. "It's fine. He was here to do a job, and he did it."

"Bullshit," she blurts out. "Just say it, Skyler. You want to rant, rave, punch something? Do it. No one would blame you."

I give her a pointed look. "Be careful there, sis, because I could say the same to you."

That has her leaning back, crossing her arms. "This is different. Your brother and I… It's complicated, and I'm not going to get his sister involved. You and Zach, gosh, Sky, it was obvious on your videos and at the hospital that he loved you."

I look down at my now cool coffee. I thought he loved me. I mean, I really felt that he loved me, but I was obviously wrong. If he loved me, he wouldn't have walked away like he did.

"Well, he's not here, Aria. He left." I suck in a breath. "I'm sorry. This is not your fault. You've been so good to me, and I appreciate you coming yesterday, but I'm fine, I really am. You should go home."

She picks up the other half of her banana bread. "I will. After I finish my snack."

Rolling my eyes, I stand up. "Okay, well, I'm going to bake."

She looks around the table that is full of banana bread, cookies, and cinnamon rolls. "More? You're going to bake more?"

I start pulling everything out of the cabinets that I need for macarons. "What can I say? Baking is soothing for me."

The worried look comes back to her face, but I wave her off. "I'm fine. This is how I process things. I'm okay."

She takes another bite, chews, and swallows. "Okay, okay. I believe you."

I line up all the ingredients. Pull out all the utensils and bowls I'm going to need. Once I have everything prepared to start, I look at my sister-in-law. "Okay, I'm going to start recording."

Aria acts as if she's zipping her lips and then motions to all the baked goods around her. "Okay, well, I'm going to just sit here, eat, and watch."

I set up the camera and then take my spot at the counter and smile into the lens.

Not because I'm happy but because I'm trying to act like I'm okay. "So today, we're making macarons. Do y'all know about macarons? They're cute, right? Flavorful. Light and tasty." I rub my belly. "Yum, am I right?"

I move through the motions. It's all standard procedure. I've done this a dozen times, so it's easy. I get lost in getting it all done.

I prepare the dry mix, make the meringue, fold the meringue into the dry mix, and then transfer the batter into the piping bag. I explain that they have to sit for an hour, and I stop the filming to wait.

Aria nods her head at me. "You're great at this, you know that, right?"

I shrug. "Yeah, well, too bad my brothers think it's just some kind of hobby or something."

Aria crosses her arms over her chest. "Sky, you bought your own house and a car. You're supporting yourself doing what you love."

I look at all the things I've baked today. Normally, I would feel fulfilled, happy, and content, but right now, I don't feel anything. I'm numb to all of it. "Yeah, well, maybe eventually my brothers will quit telling me to find a real job."

"They love you, sis. I know they can be a pain, but they love you."

I nod, thinking about my brothers. There's never been any doubt that they love me. Heck, as soon as they heard about yesterday, they all dropped everything and came to the hospital to see me. Miller was in Kentucky and chartered a helicopter to get back. Guy missed his baseball game last night because he didn't make it back in time. The Internet has been in a frenzy accusing him of everything from partying too hard, to being in rehab and other speculations. And Ozzy left right in the middle of a cattle auction to go to the hospital. Luckily, I was taken to the hospital that Penn works at, so he automatically took over my care. Yeah, I've never questioned if my family loves me. I just want them to see me as an adult, that's all. But right now, that's the least of my problems.

Aria and I talk some more. I do a few dishes and then stop when my timer goes off.

I look at the clock. "Okay, back to taping."

I turn the camera back on and go to look at the macarons. There's no hiding my disappointment. It's like it all hits me at once. I pick up one of the cookies on a spatula and hold it up to the camera. Defeated, my voice is low and flat. "All right, guys, it's been an hour, and by now the tops should be dry before baking, but they're still sticky." I poke my finger into the cookie to demonstrate how sticky they are. "Which means if I bake them now, they're likely going to explode and not rise."

I set the cookie down and look directly into the camera. "This is kind of like relationships, ya know? You can do it all, and it feels good, you're happy, and then it just falls apart when the heat hits."

Lost, I stare into the camera and then shake my head. "Anyway, this batch is probably doomed, so I'm going to call it a night. I'll try this again later… when I'm ready, but for now, I dunno. Maybe it's good to sometimes share with you my baking fails."

I blow out a breath. Everything feels so heavy right now, and before the tears start to fall, I know I should sign off. "Anyway, Cookie Crew, thanks for being here, and thanks for watching. I'll see you soon!"

I no sooner turn off the camera than the tears start to fall. Instantly, Aria is there, her arms around me, and I bury my head in her shoulder. I don't hold anything back as my body wracks with sobs.

Aria is rubbing my back, and she softly tries to soothe me. "I know, sweetie. I know it hurts. Let it all out. I'm here."

I lean into her and don't even try to hold back the tears. I couldn't if I tried. The air is filled with the scent of almonds and icing, and even in all this, I refuse to fall into the grief. The cookies on the counter are not salvageable, but maybe, just maybe, my heart still can be.

CHAPTER 21
ZACH

My phone rings, and I look at the caller ID. As soon as I see my sister's name, I know I have to answer it. "Hey, sis."

Abby sighs. "Zach Campbell, if I wasn't so worried about you, I would be yelling at you right now. Are you okay?"

I tap a pen on my desk. "Yes, I'm fine."

"Fine?" she shrills. "You're fine? You shot someone! You were—"

I cut her off. "Abby, listen, I'm okay. I was on the job."

She groans. "I know it was the Brody sister. I heard she was in the hospital. Is she okay?"

Well, the small town gossip is alive and well. "Yes, she's okay. I mean, she was hurt, but she's going to be okay."

My mind starts to race, replaying everything from yesterday, and I have to shake the thoughts out. "So uh, how are my niece and nephew? I need to come and see them."

Abby huffs. "They're fine… Zach, are you okay? I mean, you just sound, I dunno, off."

I hate it. Even with the age difference, my sister and I have always been close, and normally, I'd talk to her about this, but right now, it's too fresh. "Yeah, I'm okay. I'm just overwhelmed with… everything, but I'm okay." I hate for my sister to worry about me, and she always does. I should have called her yesterday. "I'm sorry, sis. I'm sorry I didn't call you. I'm sorry you had to hear about it from someone else. I'm sorry—"

"Stop," she says. "Stop it right now, Zach. I'm not trying to make you feel bad. I just needed to know you're okay, but it's obvious that something is bothering you."

I massage my temples. "Yeah, you're right, okay, and I promise I'll talk to you about it, but I can't… not right now… not yet."

I just can't right now. I'm barely holding it together, and I'm afraid I'll lose my shit if I start telling Abby everything.

She starts a rant. "What is it with you guys? Davis is the same way. He thinks he's gotta handle everything on his own. Like I can't handle it."

I can't help it; I laugh. "Your husband doesn't think you can't handle it. He just doesn't want you to have to handle it. He wants to take care of you."

"Zach, I'm worried about you."

I nod. "I know you are, but I'm okay, and I'll come over later this week and tell you everything."

She pauses. "I watch the Cookie Crew, bub, and I saw you on there. Was that real? Or was that part of the job?"

I blow out a rushed breath. "It was real."

"Was?" she asks.

I stare up at the white ceiling. "Yeah… was."

"Zach!" Logan hollers as he walks into our new office.

I push my chair back as I stand up. "Sis, I gotta go.

Logan just walked in. I love you, and I'll talk to you this week."

"I love you too, Zach."

I hang up as Logan calls my name again. "Zach!"

I should walk around my desk to meet him, but I stand here and wait. "In here," I call.

He walks into my office, and I take in his disheveled look. His hair is standing up in every direction, he has a few days of beard growth, and his clothes are filthy, letting me know he came here straight off the plane. "What the fuck, Zach?"

He's angry, and I don't blame him. "I know. I'm sorry. I fucked up, and I know I did." I suck in a breath and shake my head. "I think I should take a step back from Stronghold Security."

Confusion etches his face, and he throws his hands up. "Wait. What the fuck are you talking about?"

I pace across the room and look out the big window. Our office is right on Main Street, and I watch the people going about their lives while I feel like I'm drowning. "I don't know, Logan. Maybe this was a bad idea. Maybe I'm not cut out for this... Maybe I should go back to the Ghost Team."

As I peer out the window, all I keep seeing is Skyler with a blade to her neck.

I'm surprised when Logan starts to talk, and he's standing right next to me. He has his arms crossed over his chest, and he's looking outside instead of at me. "So, uh, you think this last job was a failure?"

I huff out a breath. "Fuck, yes it was. Of the biggest proportion. I failed…" I clench my eyes shut and open them again. "And this was the biggest mission… This is one I shouldn't have failed… and I did."

Logan sighs, and I hang my head. "I'm sorry, Logan, truly I am. Skyler…"

I can't even get it all out. Since Sky kicked me out of her house yesterday, I've been a mess. There's so much that needs to be done around here, but I haven't been able to focus on any of it. All I can do is worry about Skyler. Is she okay? How's her concussion? The bruise on her face? Her heart? I turn to Logan. "Have you seen her?"

He shakes his head. "No, but I talked to Aria and my brothers. What happened?"

I tense. How do I tell him that I was in Skyler's bedroom while she was downstairs being attacked? I wrap my arms around my chest. "We were in Skyler's bedroom."

Logan's jaw tightens, and his gaze pierces me. I wouldn't blame him if he hit me. "She was going down to the kitchen, and Miller called my cell. I stayed in the bedroom to talk to him while she went downstairs."

He curses. "She's my sister, Zach."

I clench my eyes. "I know."

He shrugs. "So what? You decide you'd have some fun while you were on the job? You just needed to pass the time?"

I put my hand to my chest, rubbing over my heart. "It wasn't like that, Logan. You know me, and you know I wouldn't—"

I stop because I shouldn't be defending myself. Whatever Logan wants to say or do to me at this point, it's valid, and I deserve it.

"How is she? Is she okay?"

He stares at me. "No, she's not fuckin' okay."

"Fuck, I knew I shouldn't have left. Is it her head? Is she—"

He cuts me off, taking a step toward me. "It's not her head."

My eyes jerk to his. "What is it? Fuck, I should have refused to leave. I should have stayed and—"

He points at me. "Yes, you should have stayed with her."

Stunned, I look at him, and he throws his hands up. "Look, my sister is strong. She's going to survive the stalker, the assault, all of it. What she's having trouble with is you leaving. I'm not sure what happened when I left, but I do know that right now, her heart is broken, and it's because of you." He takes a step toward me. "You hurt my sister, Zach."

I jut my chin at him. "She's better off."

He laughs darkly. "Better off how? Better off without you? Better off with some other man? How exactly is she better off?"

I lift my chin. The thought of her with another man makes me crazy. "She deserves better than me." I slap my hand to my chest. "Look at me, Logan. I couldn't even protect her. I couldn't—"

He interrupts me. "You fuckin' saved her life!"

I grit my teeth and fist my hands at my sides. "He shouldn't have been able to touch her. That's on me. That's my fault."

Logan laughs. "Zach, we've been friends for a long time, but ever since that incident in Afghanistan, you've been different. Any time you've had a chance at being happy, you've fucked it up. You act like Randall dying that day, our friends getting hurt… I don't know. You carry that shit like it was your fault. Like you were the one that set the bomb off."

I turn away from him, not wanting him to see how much just thinking about that day still devastates me. "I was the only one not hurt that day. I was—"

He throws a hand up. "You are alive and uninjured! You helped save them, Zach, but I'm tired of seeing you punish yourself, and now… Now you're punishing my sister. You think she deserves a better man? Well, I don't think there is a better man. You think I would have you protect my sister if there was someone better? I wouldn't."

He takes a deep breath and slowly lets it out. "Listen, Zach, we're partners in Stronghold, and you're not going anywhere, regardless of whether you're with my sister or not, but listen, do something for me."

I turn and look at him. "What?"

He puts his hands on his hips. "I'm going to say this, and I need you to believe me. That accident years ago was not your fault. This with my sister was not your fault. You saved her."

I want to argue with him, but I stay silent, and he continues. "Do you love my sister?"

I nod as the ache in my chest intensifies. "Yes, but—"

He doesn't let me finish. "Okay, you love her. Well, she's young, beautiful, smart, talented, she's all the things. Do you really think she's just going to be single forever? Alex told me about all the men dropping in her DMs. This is Whiskey Run. You're going to run into each other. You going to be okay seeing her with another man, seeing her pregnant with a child that's not yours?"

Anger fuels me until I see red, and I'm shaking my head. "No, no, I won't be okay with it. I'll lose my damn mind."

Logan slaps me hard on the chest. "I know you will. Figure this shit out, Campbell, and you better figure it out quick. I don't like knowing my sister is sad."

Before I can answer him, the front door jingles, letting us know someone has come in. Logan looks at me, and my stomach drops. Shit. I should have warned him. I should have prepared him for this, but I've been caught up in my own shit. "Logan—" I start just as Bree walks up to my open door.

Logan tenses next to me, and I watch as he and Bree stare at each other. Logan's voice is thick. "What the hell are you doing here?"

Bree lifts her chin and walks into the office, setting down the folders in her arms on top of my desk. "I mailed out the forms you asked me to send and opened a PO box." She looks between Logan and me. "I'll be at my desk."

Without another word, she walks out, and Logan turns to me. "What the hell was that? What's going on? What is my ex-girlfriend doing here?"

I brace myself. "I hired her."

"You did what?" he bellows.

I nod and decide to just give it all to him at once. "And there is a contract. She's guaranteed a job for a full year."

His mouth drops before snapping it shut. "You know what?" He shakes his head. He's practically trembling with emotion, and I want to tell him why I did it, but he's not ready to hear it. He holds a hand up. "I came straight from the airstrip. I need to shower and get my shit together before I do something I'm going to regret. I'm going home, Zach. I'll be in tomorrow, and hopefully, you have shit fixed by then."

I follow him through the office, and we pass Bree on the way. She's looking down at some papers on her desk as if she doesn't even see us. "I told you there's a contract, Lo. Bree is employed at Stronghold Security for a year."

He stops and glares at Bree and then back to me. "I mean my sister. Fix this with my sister." He waves his hand toward Bree. "I'll deal with her tomorrow."

He slams his way out the door, and I turn to Bree. She's still looking at the door Logan walked out of. I've wondered if I made the right decision hiring her, but seeing the look between the two of them earlier, I know I did. Whether they fix it or not, they need to deal with it. I try to reassure Bree. "It's going to be fine."

She blurts out a laugh. "No, it's not. It's going to

blow up in all our faces." She sits up a little taller. "But I can handle it."

I nod. "Okay, well, let me know if you need anything."

I walk back into my office and drop into my chair, exhaustion pulling me down. I lean my head back and close my eyes. For the first time since yesterday, it's not Skyler with a knife to her throat that I see. It's Skyler with a swollen belly, carrying a child… our child. The sight hits me hard. I want her. I want us. I may never be enough, but I will spend the rest of my days trying to be. I have to because a life without Skyler is no life at all.

CHAPTER 22
SKYLER

I take a few deep breaths. It's time for my live on ClipClap, and I've told myself all day that I'm ready for it, but now that I'm about to hit the live button, I'm not so sure.

I finally convinced Aria that I was okay. She helped me with my makeup to hide the bruise on my face, and then she went home. I spent the afternoon planning for tonight's live, and as I look at the counter, seeing all the ingredients and everything set up and ready, I try to focus. I can do this.

I take a deep breath, let it out, and then hit the button to go live. With a smile on my face, I wave at the camera. "Hey Cookie Crew! I'm here, and I'm ready to get lost in the baking. You know how when sometimes you need to take a break and do something that doesn't require a lot of thinking? That's how baking is for me."

I suck in a breath. Already, I'm off track. *Focus, Skyler.*

"All right, friends, I have a treat for you. Today, we're making an apple pie. I don't know about you, but homemade pies make me think of home, cozy, safety… love."

The word catches in my throat, and I turn away from the camera to get myself together. Maybe Aria was right; maybe this was too soon. Forcing a smile to my face, I hold up a bowl and point into it. "Okay, to start, we're going to make the dough." I mix in the flour, sugar, and salt and then add cut-up slices of butter. I mix and then add ice water until the dough comes together. I work the dough, shaping it as I instruct how to do it.

I wrap the two discs of dough in plastic and then put it in the fridge to chill.

I hold up an apple. "Okay, guys, are we having fun? Next, we're going to make the filling."

As I prepare the filling, I talk to my viewers. "So how are you guys? Everyone doing okay?" I lean in to read the comments. "Hey, Elise! Yes, apple pie is my favorite too."

"Hey, Kara, I love caramel. We can add that to the apple filling. Yum!"

My face falls as I read another comment. "Zach? Uh, he's not here."

I hold a finger up to the camera. "I'll be right back. I need to get something from the fridge."

I walk off screen, take a deep breath, and try to get myself together. I should have been prepared for this. I should have known that people would ask about Zach, and I'm not ready to answer them. It's too soon.

I lean back into the frame and smile. "And I'm back!" As I slice the apples and the thunk of the knife hitting the board fills the quiet kitchen, I start to ramble. "Like I said, I love a good apple pie. I love the smell of it baking. I mean, who doesn't love when the scent of apple and cinnamon fills your house? It's comforting, right?"

I hold up an apple. "It's weird, if you think about it. Like, I have this apple and some of them are perfect, crisp, and sweet." I hold up an apple with a big bruise on the side. "And then sometimes you get an apple with a bruise, and you have to decide if you're going to cut around the bruise and use what's left or if you should throw the whole thing out."

I pause and tighten my hold on the knife before I start slicing out the bruise. Instead of looking at the camera, I'm staring at the bruised apple as I work. "Heartbreak is kind of like that. When your heart gets bruised, you wonder if you're ever going to be whole again. You can't just cut out that bruised side of your heart, though. And yeah, people say that time heals, but in that moment, you don't believe them. You begin to wonder if you'll ever be the same again. Will the ache ever stop? Or will you always be half a person with a bruised heart?"

I let out a breath and then dump the apple slices into the bowl. "What if you just have to learn to live like this? With a heart that never heals."

I use my arm and wipe at a tear that has rolled down my cheek, and I force out a laugh. "Oh my goodness, Cookie Crew, this was supposed to be about pie."

I pick up the cinnamon as my back door opens. I freeze, and then I'm stunned when Zach walks in.

His gaze eats me up, and he points to the door. "You left the door unlocked."

I swallow, unable to form a sentence.

He moves into the room. "I was sitting in your driveway, watching your live, and I had to come in. I hope that's okay."

I nod.

"I'm sorry. I shouldn't have left. Seeing you hurt about killed me, and I convinced myself that you were better off without me."

Finally, I find my voice. "I'm not." Stronger, firmer, I shake my head. "I'm not better without you, Zach."

He walks toward me but stops short of touching me. "I'm lost without you, Skyler. I love you. I love you so much, and even though I know you deserve someone better, I can't let you go."

I clear my throat and look at the camera, my heart pounding. "Hey everyone." I chuckle. "Uh, sometimes these lives go off the rails, huh? I know we have a pie to make, but I'm going to need a few minutes. I'll be back... thirty minutes, okay?"

I lean down and look at the comments. People are screaming in all caps saying no and wondering what's going on. I turn to Zach. "They want to know if you're going to be on the live later too."

He swallows hard and nods. "Yeah, I'll be here. I'm not going anywhere."

His words hit me hard, and I look back at the camera. "All right, everyone. We're taking a short break. Make sure your notifications are turned on so you know when I come back on." I wave into the camera. "See you soon."

As soon as I turn off the live, I look at Zach. I want to forgive him, I really do, but I can't just let this go. Not yet. "What happened?"

He takes a step toward me and stops. He gestures to the camera. "I'm sorry for interrupting your live, but I was watching from the car. I was going to come in afterward, but when I saw how sad you were, I couldn't wait."

"I'm glad you did."

He lifts his arms as if he's going to reach for me and then stops and fists his hands at his sides instead. "I know I fucked up, Sky. I was stupid." He shakes his head like he's trying to get rid of thoughts. "First, I want you to know I'm sorry. I'm sorry I let you get hurt."

I stutter to get the words out. "What are you talking

about? You saved me, Zach. You didn't let me get hurt."

He nods. "I did. He shouldn't have been able to get to you."

I cut him off. "I'm the one that unlocked the door for Terry. It was my fault."

He shakes his head and comes toward me, grabbing on to my hands. "Don't say that. None of this is your fault. I will live the rest of my life knowing I let you down when you needed me, but I promise you, Sky, that if you let me, I'll spend the rest of my life making sure you never doubt that I love you, because I do. I love you more than anything."

I open my mouth, but before I can get anything out, Zach continues. "Before you decide, I should probably tell you everything."

My heart drops. I'm not sure what he's going to say, but I know he's right; I need to hear it all. "Okay," I murmur.

He holds one of my hands and puts one of his on the side of my neck. I suck in a breath. The heat of his look, the feel of his touch, all of it is just too much. He licks his lips, searching my eyes. "Sky, today, when I was thinking of you, I had this picture in my head. You were pregnant. Fuck, you were so beautiful, and in my mind, it was my baby you were carrying under your heart." He trembles and cups my cheek in his hand. "I want it all. I don't want temporary, baby. I want us. You are my everything. I dream of having my ring on your finger, building a family—a life—together."

I want all of that too, but I'm scared. Scared that he's going to change his mind or that he'll figure out I'm not what he wants.

"Zach, I want all of that… I really do, but I can't go all in and have you decide to walk away." I lift my chin. "You broke me when you ended this, when you treated me like a job, and I don't know if I'll survive it again. I want to trust you…"

He leans forward, pressing his forehead to mine. It's like I can feel the emotion inside him wrapping around us. He lifts his head, kisses my forehead, and steps back. "I'll give you all the time you need, but I'm not leaving you again, Sky, and I promise you that I'll spend the rest of my life proving that to you."

I lift my hands, curling my fingers into his shirt. "Don't make promises—"

He tilts his head. "Don't make promises I can't keep?" He gives me a reassuring look. His voice is firm and self-assured. "I'm keeping every promise I make to you. Let me prove it to you."

I put my hands on his shoulders. "How about we start with a kiss…"

He puts his hands at my waist, pulling me flush to his body. "I'm in. I'm all in."

As soon as our lips touch, something inside me unravels. I melt against him as he deepens the kiss. The feel of him pressed against me, the way he holds me like he never wants to let me go is freeing in a way I've never felt before.

With my heart pounding, I force myself to pull back even though it's the last thing I want to do. "Thank you for coming back, Zach. I know I told you to go… "

He shakes his head. "I'm here now, and I'm not going anywhere."

With a shaky smile and a racing heart, I smile. "Good. Because we have a pie to finish."

CHAPTER 23
ZACH

I love being with Skyler in her home. Just being with her makes me happy. I can't believe I thought I could stay away from her, but I wasn't lying when I told her I wanted forever.

I clap my hands together. "Okay, so uh, apple pie… you know I have no idea what I'm doing, right?"

She points to the table. "You can sit and watch if you want to."

I put a hand at her waist. "I'd like to help, but if that's going to mess you up, then I can sit and watch."

She giggles, and it's the best sound. "No, I'd love for you to help me." She points at the camera. "You're going to be on my ClipClap channel. The world is going to see you."

I nod. "Yeah, well, I just told the world that I love you."

Her eyes light up. "You think my brothers were watching?"

I shrug, not worried in the least. Nothing and no one is going to stop me from being with Skyler. "I'd say they probably know by now."

She gets the dough out of the refrigerator and sets it down on the counter in front of me. "Okay, when I turn the camera on, you're going to roll out the dough."

Instead of looking down, I'm looking at her. The curve of her cheek, her full lips, her big blue eyes. She catches me staring. "What are you looking at?"

I tell her the truth. "I'm just happy to be here with you."

Her whole face lights up, and I love to see it.

She points at the camera. "I'm going to go live. You ready?"

I nod. "I'm ready."

She hits Go Live and then smiles into the camera. "Okay, everyone. We're back! I'm going to give everyone a few minutes to get on, and then we're going to get started."

She starts reading comments. "Hey, Kara! I'm glad you're back. Yes, I'm good."

I can't look away from Skyler. She's smiling, reading the comments, and I relax a little because seeing her happy is all I want.

She stands next to me. "Okay, so I have my helper here. Everyone say hi to Zach. He's going to roll out the dough."

She instructs me how to do it, and I roll it out, careful and even.

She talks to her viewers as I roll the dough, and I'm really trying to concentrate on what I'm doing, but it's hard when all I want to do is look at Skyler.

"Oh, good question." She looks at me and winks. "Yes, Zach is my boyfriend."

My chest puffs out. Fuck yeah, I am.

I lean in to look at the screen and see a few messages.

"OMG, he's cute!"

"Zach and Skyler forever!"

I read the commenter's name and address her out loud. "Yes, Rachel, I like the way you think. Zach and Skyler forever."

Skyler bites her lip, trying to contain her smile.

She hip-checks me. "Okay, so I'm going to lay out the dough for the crust. Then we'll fill it and then you can lay over the top crust. What do you think?"

I take a deep breath. "Let's do it."

She makes it look easy. She lays out the dough in the pie dish and works it in, then she pours in the apple filling. She points at me. "Okay, your turn."

I pick up the flattened pie crust. I'm much more awkward about it, but I get it done. She claps her hands together. "Good job, Zach. That's perfect."

I couldn't stop smiling if I tried, and I kiss her forehead. "It's because I have a great teacher."

She picks up an egg and cracks it into a small bowl. I stir it with the brush, and she nods her head. "Yes, just paint that right on the crust."

I do as she's instructed, and when I'm done, she picks up the pie. "Can you open the oven?"

I open it up, and she puts it in. "Okay, Cookie Crew, you put it in the oven at three hundred and seventy-five degrees for about an hour."

She grabs my hand, and I step toward the camera. I stand behind her, loving the way she leans into me. "Okay, so this is going to bake, and I'm going to sign off. Thank you so much for being here. I'll post some pictures for you tomorrow of the finished product."

She waves at the camera and then squeezes my hand, and I wave too. "See you next time, Cookie Crew."

She hits the end button, and when she stands up, she's smiling at me. "You realize that video had more viewers than I've ever had, and I don't think they were here for the baking."

I cup her cheek. "They were here for you, honey. They just wanted to see you smiling."

She looks at the oven and back at me. "So, uh, what are we going to do for an hour?"

I don't dare get my hopes up. I know exactly what I want to do, but I'm not going to pressure her into anything. I suck in a breath. "What do you want to do?"

She loops her arms around my neck, and her breasts smash against my chest. "I have some ideas."

I look into her eyes. "I want you, Skyler. There's no doubt about that." I press my hips toward her, and her eyes widen when she feels the hard bulge press into her belly. "But I can wait. I didn't come here for that… I just need to be with you."

She pats a hand against my chest. "I want to, Zach. I want to feel close to you."

I don't hesitate. I pick her up and hold her in my arms. Without a second thought, I carry her up the stairs to her bedroom. I pause in the doorway, my heart hammering. Excitement builds inside me until my body trembles with it. This time feels different. This feels like forever.

"What's wrong? Why did you stop?"

My heart is pounding. There's heat in my chest, and I feel as if I'm struggling to form words. "I love you, Skyler."

She smiles. "Show me. Show me how you love me."

She makes it sound like a challenge, and I walk into the room, kicking the door shut behind us. "With pleasure, baby."

EPILOGUE

SKYLER

Three Months Later

There's a knock on the door, and I look over at Zach. He just smiles widely at me without any surprise on his face.

"Who could that be?" I ask, surprised. We're about to go live for the Sweet Temptations channel, and we don't have much time.

Zach's smile gets even bigger. "I'll go see."

I watch him walk out of the kitchen, and I know something is up. He's been acting weird all day, but no matter how many times I ask, he says nothing.

The last three months have been amazing. Zach has been busy getting Stronghold Security started, but he comes home every night. I've thought about talking to him about letting his apartment go, but I didn't want to be presumptuous or anything.

"Look who's here!" Zach walks back into the kitchen followed by my brothers Miller, Logan, Guy, Ozzy, and Penn, and my sister-in-law, Aria.

"Oh my God! What are you all doing here? What's going on?"

The guys all take turns hugging me, and when I get to Aria, she holds me extra tight. "Love you, sis."

She sniffles as if she's going to cry, and I pat her shoulder, "I love you, too." I'm starting to get freaked out. "You guys! What are you doing here?"

Zach is the first one to answer. "They wanted to be here for the taping of Baking with Zach! Is that okay?"

My mouth drops. For years, my brothers have discredited my baking as a real job. It seems like forever they wanted me to do a job that offers more security. It was only when my followers increased and I was booking segments on television shows and getting orders for big parties that they thought I could make something of this. It also doesn't hurt that Zach has been on my side since the day we met and sings my praises at every turn. I sniff, wanting to cry now. "Yes, I would love that! Okay, does everyone want to grab a chair? We're going to get started soon and—"

The doorbell rings again, and I'm shocked when Zach leans down and kisses my forehead. "Two more. I'll be right back."

"Two more?" I put my hands on my hips. "What is going on, you guys?"

I look around at my brothers, but they're all just smiling at me. Zach comes back into the kitchen, followed by his sister and brother-in-law. "Sky, Abby and Davis wanted to come too." He holds his hands up. "But this is it. Promise."

My kitchen is full, and my heart is about to explode. Abby and Davis both hug me and then find some seats that Zach has produced from somewhere. I ask Abby, "Where are Alexis and DJ? They could have come!"

Abby laughs. "Maybe next time. They would have wanted to bake with Aunt Sky instead of sitting to watch."

My heart warms instantly. From the first time Zach took me to his sister's house, she's been amazing and instantly started referring to me as Aunt Sky.

"We're just missing your mom and dad and everyone would be here," I tell Zach.

He nods. "Don't worry. They're watching from the cruise ship!"

With my hand to my heart, I suck in an emotional breath and look around at our family. I can't believe they all came here tonight. They all know we're starting a new segment for my channel, but I never dreamed we would get this kind of support. "I can't tell you how much it means that you guys came tonight. I love that you're here." I look at Zach and poke my finger into his stomach. "This means you're going to have to share the baked goods."

He looks stricken and then shrugs. "I guess I can share for one night." He claps his hands together. "Okay, it's time to get started."

I smile at our family as Zach and I take our places behind the counter. I look up at Zach. "You ready for this?"

He chuckles and rubs his hands together. "Yes, I'm ready. So ready." He leans down and kisses me, and instead of just a peck on the lips, he kisses me until

I'm breathless and my brothers are all calling out, "Okay, okay, enough of that."

I giggle as Zach pulls back. My brothers were hesitant when we first started dating, but Zach has completely won them over.

Zach hugs me to him. "Okay, okay, down to business." He leans over the phone. "You ready?"

I wave a hand at my overheated face. "Yes, as ready as I'll ever be."

He winks at me and presses the button to record.

Zach holds my hand as we both look into the camera. I'm doing my best to concentrate, but it's a little hard as our brothers and sisters are all staring at us with big smiles on their face. I focus on the camera. "Hey, Cookie Crew! Do we have a treat for you tonight! I love how excited you all are for this new segment for Sweet Temptations! This is our first 'Baking with Zach' segment, and we're going to be making my personal favorite: fudgy ooey gooey brownies!"

Zach smacks his lips and rubs his tummy. "Yummy!"

I look up at him with a smile on my face. "You're excited about this one, aren't you?"

He has a twinkle in his eye. "More than you know."

His voice has dropped, and it's that tone he uses when he's close, making me wild for him. I remind myself that I'm on camera and all five of my brothers are in the room. Clearing my throat, I nod to our family. "But before we get started, I wanted to tell you that we have some visitors tonight."

I walk around and pick up the camera and then turn it on our family. "Look who's here! My five brothers, my sister-in-law, and Zach's sister and brother-in-law! We have a full house tonight."

Zach pops in next to me with a frown on his face. "And she's making me share the brownies with them."

We both laugh, and Zach takes the camera from my hand, holding it up so he's the focal point. "But first, there's something I need to do."

He hands the camera to my brother Logan, who turns it toward Zach and me. Zach goes down on one knee. I gasp, putting my hands up to my mouth.

He shakes his head, his gaze completely on me. He opens a ring box and holds it up to me, his voice shaky when he speaks. "Baby, the moment I watched the video Logan sent me of you where you were making s'mores, I knew in that moment I wanted you to be my wife. Skyler, you're beautiful, you're smart, you're talented, and you're a light to anyone that knows you. For three months, I wanted to ask you this, and I don't want to wait one more day. I love you, Skyler, and every day I spend with you, I love you more. You make me happier than I've ever been, and I want to spend the rest of my life with you. Will you please do me the honor of becoming my wife?"

It amazes me that he's nervous, but now I can see that's what was off with him today. He has to know I'm going to say yes. "Yes, Zach, yes, I'll marry you."

He takes the ring out of the box and slides it on my finger. He stands up to his full height, lifting me into his arms, and swings me around. He holds me tightly, and I melt into his arms. We kiss, and even though I don't want to, I pull away. "I love you, Zach."

He rests his head against mine. "I love you too, baby." He leans down to whisper in my ear, "We're going to celebrate tonight."

My whole body starts to tremble in anticipation. Reluctantly, he pulls back and points to our family. Miller comes forward first, and then everyone else does. Logan has stopped recording, and everyone in the room takes turns congratulating us. The whole time, Zach holds my hand as if he doesn't want to let me go.

Zach kisses my head. "I'm going to grab some of your treats." He pulls out the cupcakes we made this morning, cookies from last night, and then pitchers of sweet tea and lemonade. Abby helps him, and I get teary-eyed when brother and sister hug each other.

Zach is quick to return to my side. "Whatever you want, baby. We can still film the segment tonight."

I'm quick to shake my head. "Nope, we're going to celebrate together, and then we're kicking our family to the curb, and me and you are going to celebrate, big guy."

Logan groans and covers his ears. "Oh my God, please, I don't need or want that image in my head."

I wiggle my eyebrows at Logan. "What? You're just going to have to get used to it, bub, because we're going to make you an uncle again as soon as we can."

I freeze, realizing what I just said out loud, and look up at Zach. "I mean, ya know, we should probably talk about it."

Zach looks at me with pure passion. His whole body is tense as if just the thought of having a baby makes him crazy. "Everyone out. Grab a cookie, grab a cupcake, but get out."

I gasp. "Zach!"

He picks me up and tosses me over his shoulder and starts walking out of the kitchen. "Thank you all for coming, but we're going to celebrate!"

Miller hollers after us, "That's my baby sister!"

I lift a hand and wave at them. "Bye, everyone. Thanks for coming tonight. We love you! Lock up on your way out."

We get upstairs, and Zach tosses me onto the bed. I sit up. "Zach, what are you thinking? They're going to know... I mean, they're going to think..."

He kicks off his shoes and pulls off his shirt, tossing it across the room. He shrugs. "This is on you, sweets. You started talking about having a baby, and I went a little crazy."

He hovers over me, and I put my arms around his neck. "So… so you want to have a baby?"

He nods. "Yes. Yes, I do."

I pull him down to me. "Okay."

His eyes widen. "Okay? You mean—?"

I push him onto his back and hover over him. "I mean, okay. I'll stop taking the pill."

He shivers, his hands gripping my hips and holding me to him. "I love you, Sky, and I want to get married tomorrow."

I gasp. "Tomorrow?"

He blows a breath. "Okay… soon. I want you to have your dream wedding, but we're doing it quick. I want my ring on your finger."

I raise up, lifting my shirt up my body and then dropping it onto the floor, and then take off my bra. "Two weeks."

His eyebrows skyrocket, and he leans up, wrapping his arms around my waist. "Two weeks? Are you sure? I want you to have the wedding you want."

I laugh. "The wedding I want is with you. Two weeks, Zach."

He kisses me then, rolling me to my back, and when he pulls away, he searches my eyes. "I promise you, Sky, you won't ever regret this."

I put my hand on the side of his face. "I know I won't. I love you, Zach, and I want forever with you."

He kisses me like he wants forever too. And for the first time, forever feels real.

———

EPILOGUE 2

ZACH

Three Months Later

As soon as I walk into the house, a warm feeling comes over me. The scent of cinnamon and sugar fills the air. "Honey, I'm home!"

I barely get the door shut when Skyler is coming toward me. She has her hair up in a top knot, her apron is covered in flour, and she's smiling ear to ear. She runs to me, and I catch her easily. "Ooh, I like this kind of welcome."

She kisses my face, quick, tiny kisses, and I wrap my arms around her as she brings her legs around my waist. I moan against her lips. "Fuck," I groan.

I carry her to the couch and sit down with her in

my lap. I reach for the hem of her shirt, but she stops me. "Wait."

I stop instantly but groan. She's holding my wrists and smiling so that her whole face is lit up. She's excited about something. I lean in and kiss the tip of her nose because I can't resist touching or kissing her. "How long am I waiting for?"

She bounces from my lap and stands up, still holding on to my hands. "Just a few minutes. I made you something special, and I want you to see it first."

I hesitate. "What is it?"

Sometimes she surprises me with a special pastry. She's surprised me with sleepovers where we've cared for my niece and nephew. She's surprised me with a hunting trip with her brothers, and all of those have been amazing, but right now the only surprise I want is some quality one-on-one time with my wife.

She puts her hands on her hips. "I promise you that this is a surprise you want."

She reaches for me, grabs my hand, and pulls me from the couch before prancing away from me. She has on my favorite shorts that show off the curve of her hips, and I reach for her, pulling her back against my chest as I walk with her to the kitchen. She stops next to the stove, and I look around for the surprise. The oven is off. The counters are clean, and I don't see anything out of the ordinary.

I rub my hands together. "What is it?"

She tilts her head up. "Guess."

I put a finger to my chin and play along with her game. "You made me something special."

She seems to think about it. "Uh, you can say that."

I nod and reach for the cookie jar, but surprisingly it's empty, so I reach for her. "You want to get naked in the kitchen?"

She giggles. "Maybe after your surprise."

I run my hands down her body, pulling her to me. "You're killing me here, sweets. Give me my surprise, and then I'll give you—"

She interrupts me with a smack to my chest. "Zach... okay. I'll give you a hint."

I palm her ass. "What's the hint?"

She puts a hand on the cold stove. "It's in the oven."

I look at her quizzically. I take one hand off her and then open the oven door. I peer inside, and on the rack is a bun. It takes me a second, but as soon as I get it, I feel the blood rush from my head, my heart starts to race, and I reach for Sky. "Really? You're pregnant? We're going to have a baby?"

She nods her head as a tear rolls down her cheek. "I was with Abby today, and I was lightheaded and a little nauseous and—"

"What? You're sick? You didn't tell me." I quickly pick her up off her feet and set her on the counter. She puts her hands on my shoulders to reassure me. "I'm fine, Zach. I promise."

I nod, caging her in with my arms, and she continues her story. "Anyway, your sister told me I should take a pregnancy test, and I did. We're having a baby."

I'm in complete awe. "We're having a baby. You're going to be a mom, and I'm going to be a dad."

She giggles. "Yes, we are."

I know my voice is shaking, but I don't care. I drop to my knees in front of her and press my cheek to her belly. "Hey, little one. I already love you."

Skyler runs her hands through my hair and sighs happily.

I keep talking, wanting to say it all. I'm not sure how I got this life. After everything I've been through, I never dreamed this was possible, but being with Skyler makes everything seem possible. "I promise I'm going to love you, protect you, and always be here for you."

Sky hugs me to her. "You're going to be the best dad."

I stand up and kiss her. Like always, the kiss goes from soft to heavy and filled with passion in an instant. When I pull away, I breathe against her lips, "Best. Surprise. Ever!"

She reaches up and wipes the tears from under my eyes. "I love you, Zach."

I pick her up. "I love you too, baby. So much."

"Forever?" she whispers.

I nod with a teary smile and a voice filled with promise. "Forever."

ALSO BY HOPE FORD

Want more of Whiskey Run?

Whiskey Run

Faithful - He's the hot, say-it-like-it-is cowboy, and he won't stop until he gets the woman he wants.

Captivated - She's a beautiful woman on the run... and I'm going to be the one to keep her.

Obsessed - She's loved him since high school and now he's back.

Seduced - He's a football player that falls in love with the small town girl.

Devoted - She's a plus size model and he's a small town mechanic.

Whiskey Run: Savage Ink

Virile - He won't let her go until he puts his mark on her.

Torrid - He'll do anything to give her what she wants.

Rigid - If you love reading about emotionally wounded men and the women that help them overcome their past, then you'll love Dawson and Emily's story.

Whiskey Run: Cowboys Love Curves

Obsessed Cowboy - She's the preacher's daughter and she's off limits.

Whiskey Run: Heroes

Ransom - He's on a mission he can't lose.

Redeem - He's in love with his sister's best friend.

Submit - She's his fake wife but he wants to make it real.

Forbid - They have a secret romance but he's about to stake his claim.

Whiskey Run: Sugar

One Night Love - Her one night stand wants more.

Rebound Love - She's falling for the rebound guy.

Second Chance Love - He is not a man to ignore... especially when he asks for a second chance.

Bad Boy Love - He's a bad boy that wants her good.

Whiskey Run: Guardians MC

Protective Biker - She needs his protection and he'll give it to her. But he's going to need her heart in exchange.

Broken Biker - There's only one woman for him...

Relentless Biker - He won't stop until he has her back.

Whiskey Men

Reluctant Husband - If you love reading about curvy women getting the hot guy, opposites attract, jealousy trope, marriage of convenience, and small-town romance, then you'll love Lucas and Isabella's story.

Something Real - If you love reading billionaire, single father, age gap, boss/employee, and small-town romance, then you'll love Ford and Lilian's story.

Coming Home - If you love reading billionaire, ex-military, age gap, forced proximity, and small-town romance, then you'll love Hudson and Elle's story.

Forever Mine - If you love reading billionaire, age gap, second chance, and small-town romance, then you'll love Beau and Natalie's story.

Always Yours - If you love reading billionaire, friends to lovers, pregnancy, and small town romance, then you'll love Austin and Ally's story.

JOIN ME!

JOIN MY NEWSLETTER

www.AuthorHopeFord.com/Subscribe

BE A HOTTIE!

JOIN HOPE'S HOTTIES ON FACEBOOK

www.FB.com/groups/hopeford

A place to talk about Hope Ford's books! Find out about new releases, giveaways, get exclusive content, see covers before anyone else and more!

ABOUT THE AUTHOR

USA Today Bestselling Author Hope Ford writes short, steamy, sweet romances. She loves tattooed, alpha men, instant love stories, and ALWAYS happily ever afters.

To find me on Pinterest, Instagram, Facebook, Goodreads, and more:

www.AuthorHopeFord.com/follow-me

Want FREE BOOKS?
Go to www.authorhopeford.com/freebies